THE
CRYING JESUS

THE CRYING JESUS

R.P. MACINTYRE

For Colleen F.

All the Best!

[signature] Mar '98

THISTLEDOWN PRESS LTD.

Canadian Cataloguing in Publication Data
MacIntyre, R. P. (Roderick Peter), 1947-
The crying Jesus
ISBN 1-895449-70-7
I. Title.
PS8575.I67C76 1997   C813'.54   C97-920118-7
PR9199.3.M322C76 1997

Book design by A.M. Forrie
Set in 11 pt. New Baskerville
by Thistledown Press Ltd.

Printed and bound in Canada by
Veilleux Impression à Demande
Boucherville, Quebec

Thistledown Press Ltd.
633 Main Street
Saskatoon, Saskatchewan
S7H 0J8

We acknowledge the support of the Canada Council for the Arts for our
publishing program. Thistledown Press also gratefully acknowledges the
continued support of the Saskatchewan Arts Board.

We write for our dead. – S.V.

The airport slough was a small lake in those days and ran from there south past Rusholme Road, more than thirty blocks in springtime. My cousin Johnny drowned in that slough. He made me a stick with a wheel attached when I was five. It was my favourite toy. I dedicate this little book to his memory.

ACKNOWLEDGEMENTS

The author acknowledges all those voices living inside his head — as well as a few who live outside it: Sharyn, of course, who lives in both places; Paddy O'Rourke, for blessing him; Seán Virgo, for phrasing those careful questions; Scott Miller, for being that first eye and all those young people for being the mirror.

The author also wishes to express his thanks for the generous contributions of the Saskatchewan Arts Board, the Canada Council and their staffs, without whose help all this would be moot.

A version of "The Front Step" appeared in *Grain* magazine.

CONTENTS

BODY PARTS

I've counted my fingers and toes. I appear to be all here. But inside me there are great gaping holes and I don't know what they are. I don't know how to fill them.

"You're so naive," said Shawna.

"What do you mean?"

"You walk around like everything is eggs, like I'm an egg."

"What do you want?" I asked.

"Don't you know?"

"No."

"I have a body you know."

"Yeah. It's a beautiful body. What's wrong with your body?"

"You have no idea."

"About what?"

"Oh, just leave me alone!" she said and stomped off, her hair flailing about her head.

Shawna dumped me. I'm bewildered. I'm crushed. She is right — I have no idea why this has happened.

We've had the perfect relationship. We get along — *got* along — talking for hours about it all: the real meaning of ambiguous song lyrics, our teachers' quirks, what really is inside an atom, the nature of God — even our families — Shawna, her strange father, and me, my odd little brother, Matt. We've talked and understood. What more is there?

On top of this, Grandma dies.

Mom says that she feels like an orphan — abandoned and alone. She's forty years old and it's hard to think of her that way. She has me, Dad and my brother — not to mention Uncle John and the rest of our extended family. But that's what she says. Her dad died when she was ten.

It's not that I'm overjoyed that my grandfather has been dead for thirty years and that I never knew him, nor does it particularly thrill me that we planted Grandma last week, but there is an upside: I'm free. I'm free and Grandpa's will gets executed.

Grandma lived on the farm till the day she died, in fact, *including* the day she died. It was the day after Shawna left me that Grandma toppled off the top of a grain truck. Nobody's quite sure what she was doing up there — possibly waving Uncle John to come in for lunch — but everyone says that it was a pretty stupid way to go, living as long as she did.

"She had another ten years in her," said Uncle John, his eyes wet. "She was only 78." He didn't mean it the way it sounded, as though she was a piece of farm equipment that expired before the due date. But he will miss her more than anyone because she ran the farm with him.

Of course now Uncle John may be able to go out and find a life outside the farm, if he's interested in such a thing, or if he knows how. He pretty much lived under Grandma's thumb and did everything that Grandma told him to, including not touch the 1952 Chev pickup that sat for thirty years under a canvas tarp in the old horse barn. The grandfather-I-never-knew parked it there.

It was Grandpa's dying wish that the contents of the horse barn go to his first grandson.

That would be me.

The contents of the old horse barn are pretty limited. Thirty years ago, it contained horses and tack as well as the truck. But the horses have long since been rendered into glue, binding the covers to some forgotten books gathering dust on a library shelf, or maybe holding wallpaper from peeling off some plaster walls. Anyway, the horses are no longer available. Their tack is hung on spikes, brittle as burnt toast. There are plenty of cobwebs, dust and ancient straw.

There is also a complication.

That would be my little brother, Matthew.

Matthew is a goofy obnoxious ten-year old. His ears are too big for his head; his nose is too small; his hair dips and bends across his skull like a late wheat field after a hail storm. He has developed the ability to belch at will. Of this, he's very proud. His specialty though, is making sound effects — not just any sound effects, but the sounds of *things breaking*. Destruction. He is very good at this.

However, Matthew is jealous: if I should get the contents of the old horse barn, left for me by a grandfather-I-never-knew, then what does Matthew get? The truth is, nothing, not so much as a spore of straw mould. So, I feel sorry for him. I promise Matthew he can have anything in the old horse barn that's not directly attached to the truck.

"Anything?" he bleats.

"Anything," I assure him.

Matthew's ecstatic. He makes all his exploding sounds at once and throws in a couple of belches for good measure. He's so happy that I begin to worry. What if he finds something worthwhile, something valuable? What if the real treasure lies hidden beneath the straw mould? I realize too that if it is there, he will find it. He's just that way. I try to think of ways to renege on my promise. I draw a blank. I'm doomed.

Uncle John accompanies us to the old horse barn. He'll help remove the tarp. Mom has stayed at the house to sort through Grandma's things and do whatever it is that parents do when their parents leave them orphaned at forty. I realize I should be sad on this occasion, but as we yank at the tarp and a great cough of thirty-year old dust heaves through the air, I'm transfixed by what's revealed.

Yes, it's true that the apple green '52 Chevy pickup sits on four flat tires, that it's missing a left front fender and a grill, that the battery has been dead longer than the horses who once shared the barn with its battered chassis and that the gas in the tank (and presumably carburetor) has devolved into some kind of prehistoric sludge. But other than that, it's a thing of beauty — perfect. Uncle John hands me a set of plates and the registration. "Graduation gift," he says to me.

Matthew has noticed little, if any, of this. He's busy scouring the old horse barn for hidden treasures. However, except for the tattered remains of old traces, halters, collars and a dead saddle, he finds nothing. He's depressed — glum. He can't even manage a half-hearted belch. Secretly, I'm pleased.

Meanwhile, Uncle John is determined to see if we can resurrect the truck from its state of suspended animation. It's no problem filling the tires with air and replacing the battery. The hard part is removing the gas tank, cleaning it — along with the carburetor — and putting it back together. We change the oil and whatever it was that acted as coolant in the heater core. All of this takes most of the afternoon and evening.

Matthew alternates between whining and throwing clumps of whatever he can find at the divebombing swallows who are upset at the invasion of their personal space. Whateverhecanfind turns out to be thirty-year old horse turds that shower us when they break across the rafters of the old horse barn. We are not pleased. We tell him so. He then proceeds to disassemble all the horse tack into its component parts — bits of dry leather, which he discards, and tarnished rings of nickel and brass. These he shines and puts into piles.

It's the moment of truth. It's time to start the old truck. I climb into the driver's seat. I turn on the ignition. Nothing. Uncle John points out that on vehicles of this vintage, the starter is a button on the panel. I push it. The truck shudders, grinds, coughs, hacks and belches smoke — it might explode. Matthew is impressed. It horks into life. The truck is running. We cheer.

I pull the light switch — the lights work. I pull the windshield wiper switch — the wipers work. I pull the heater fan switch — nothing much happens. The fan seems clogged and stiff. I turn it on "high". It whirs reluctantly and a strange red mist flies up onto the windshield.

"Cool," says Matthew.

"What is it?" I ask.

"I think it's blood," says Uncle John.

It *is* blood.

We have puréed a nest of mice into oblivion. By midnight, we have dismantled the heater system.

The next morning at breakfast, Matthew is doing his impression of the truck starting.

"Matthew," says Mom.

"What?" says Matthew.

"Cut it out," says Dad.

"I'm not doing anything," says Matthew.

"Eat your breakfast," says Mom.

"I am," says Matthew. "Can I look at the dead mice?"

"No," they both say with their volume turned up.

"There's not much to see," I say. "Just red gorp."

"Yeah?" Matthew's eyes go wide.

"Yeah. Mixed with fur and nest stuff."

"Cool," says Matthew.

"Matthew!" Mom and Dad repeat.

"I didn't do anything!"

"Eat your breakfast — you too, Jesse," says Dad.

"I don't get *anything*," shrieks Matthew.

I now feel sorry for Matthew. He *doesn't* get anything; he doesn't even get to see what's left of the dead mice. All he has are a few brass rings. I decide in a fit of guilt to take him to a movie. It's one of those *Disney* animated movies, a translation of some classic literature I haven't read and probably never will read. Our parents hold a public debate on how the experience will likely rot our minds, so we are both quite eager to see it.

We're standing in line at the movie. Matthew is trying to learn how to fart at will. Unfortunately his failures leave brown stains in his shorts. I warn him that standing in line for a movie or sitting in a movie theatre is not the place to practice this. He doesn't seem to hear me because he's gawking at something behind us. I turn to look.

Standing not two feet from me is an astonishingly beautiful woman who looks about my age and appears to glow in broad daylight. She blinks, once, calmly, with the biggest, softest, darkest almond-shaped eyes and turns the corners of her mouth up, ever so slightly. This is the moment when I forget completely about Shawna. I'm cooked.

I'm in love. It's instant, like being hit by a truck. "Cause of Love Instant," say the headlines. "He didn't have a chance," say onlookers. I gather my gaping eyeballs, close my gaping mouth and try to turn around. Matthew, however, is still gawking.

"Matthew," I try to say without moving my lips, "don't stare." It's not fair that he should get to stare and I don't.

"How does she blow her nose?" he bleats.

The entire lineup to the movie turns around. Well, perhaps one or two people. One of them is me.

I hadn't noticed in that first instant, but the beautiful woman who looks about my age is wearing a nose ring — a tiny silver nose ring.

"Don't ask stupid questions," I hiss at Matthew.

From behind me comes a silvery laugh. It's her. She's laughing at me.

"Like this," I hear a voice behind me say.

Right then and there she gives Matthew a demonstration on how you blow your nose wearing a nose ring. I'm too humiliated to watch. But Matthew is all eyes.

"Cool," he says, and with this mystery unlocked, he feels free to roam, to check out the posters for upcoming movies.

If sheep smile, I'm smiling like one. "My little brother," I say, acknowledging responsibility for the uncouth youth perusing posters. And picking his nose. I'm hoping he doesn't eat it. He has stopped in front of a "Coming Soon" movie featuring exploding body parts.

"He has nice eyes," she says.

I have never looked at Matthew's eyes the way a woman might look at them. It occurs to me that they are one physical trait we happen to share and that this might be an indirect compliment. I stammer something profound like, "Yeah." I want to say, *So do you,* but that would be too direct, too true. Too incriminating.

I'm not strong around women. I'm much more comfortable around machines — cars, trucks, even computers. You can get your hands or your brain on them. On women, all you can get is your eyes. You can look and wonder.

For example, you can wonder what the heck she's doing here. Most of the lineup is littered with young children and mothers — older women in their thirties. There aren't many who look my age. In fact, there is only the one, and she's standing behind me wearing a nose ring. I'm wondering about this when Matthew does the inevitable: he pops something from his nose into his mouth. I shudder.

"Are you alone?" a voice behind me asks.

It's her. I shudder again. I'm beginning to feel slightly nauseous. "Ah, well no," I manage to stutter.

"I mean, besides your brother."

"No."

This comes out much too loud. It sounds like *no, go away,* when really I mean, *no, I'm very alone, I couldn't be more alone — except for my brother.*

"Do you mind if I sit with you?" she asks.

"No." This time the word sort of squeaks out of me like I'm a rubber ducky.

"Thanks," she says, "I prefer sitting with children — boy children."

I suppose my eyebrows raise at this. I suppose I'm vaguely insulted or hurt. I suppose she sees this.

"Your brother," she adds, "I mean, you're an adult," she says, making things altogether murky. But I'm glad she's flustered. It makes her human.

By this time, Matthew is back. He's gawking again. This time at her midriff. She's wearing a sweater that exposes that part of her body. I surreptitiously glance in that direction. Another silver ring adorns her navel.

"Shut up," I snap, just as Matthew opens his mouth to speak.

Graciously, uncharacteristically, he obeys.

✦✦✦

Now, to say this might be the beginning of a beautiful relationship would be too easy, too simple. I'm finding out that life is just not that way. It's true that Jennifer, glowing Jennifer, is studying animation, which is why she's going to a *Disney* movie, and it's true she instantly likes Matthew, despite himself, and she thinks I'm a fine upstanding example of how older brothers should behave towards their younger siblings. But there are a couple of other truths as well: the first is she has a boyfriend. The second is she's twenty-two: she's getting up there. I'm only seventeen.

She has taken to coming over. My parents are perplexed. They preferred Shawna.

Not only is Jennifer older than me and wears hardware in various body parts, but Matthew behaves like a human being when she's around. She draws him pictures, cartoons, and little portraits.

"Doesn't it hurt?" Matthew asks.

"What hurt?" asks Jennifer.

"Them rings," says Matthew.

"No, of course not. I wouldn't do it if it hurt."

Matthew looks disappointed. For a second. He brightens with a new thought.

"Could I do it?"

"Do what?"

"Get rings."

"I don't know. You'll have to ask your mom." She touches him on the head. She never touches me. Physically.

Matthew disappears into the kitchen. He's not gone a moment, when a very loud, "No! Definitely not!" explodes from the room.

Orphans are so rigid.

+++

Uncle John and I have very nearly reassembled the truck heater, having scoured both it and the windshield of dead mice. The windshield is actually two plates of glass divided in the middle. The passenger side has a spider web crack now infused with a darkened, slightly rust-tinged stain, the exact same colour as our back deck. I now think of mice, or blood, or some combination of the two, every time I step outside. But the truck is pretty well ready for the road, in fact has been on the road, from the farm to our driveway — minus a fender and a grill, of course.

The farm is only a few miles out of town and Uncle John doesn't seem to like spending as much time there as he did when he shared the place with Grandma. So, he spends it here. Maybe he too feels orphaned. Or maybe it's Grandma's ghost haunting him. Or maybe it's her minty scent still lingering, making him sad. Or maybe he just doesn't know what to do next without Grandma there to tell him.

Grandma did strange things. She would take her teeth out at meal time, rinse them off in the sink and place them beside her on the table. Appetizing. She would make soup out of chicken feet and tea out of weeds. "It's good for you," she would say. The tea smelt like mint. Then she would cook fish. "Brain food," she would say. Grandma: no teeth, minty fish and chicken feet.

At any rate, Uncle John is Mom's younger brother, somewhere in his late thirties. For all his chicken feet and fish eating, you'd think he'd be a genius, but he's not. He seems lost. When he met Jennifer for the first time, he nodded at her, got up and went outside to bolt a new fender onto the truck. I helped. All she had done was blink once, calmly with her big sad sleepy slanty eyes, and smile.

"Why is she spending so much time here?" Mom asks.

"Who?" I say.

"You know very well who," she says.

Of course I know well who. I'm just stalling for time, trying to think of a good answer, a good lie, a *believable* lie. Or even the truth if I knew what it was.

"All she does is sit here and draw," says Mom.

"Well that's not all," I say, "she talks to Matthew."

He enters on cue. He has a handful of brass rings, the ones from the horse tack.

"Hey, listen to this," he says. A long, slippery fart fills the room — the sound of one; the smell will follow.

"Matthew! Your brother and I are trying to have a conversation here!"

"About what?" he asks.

"Never you mind. Go play outside."

"Can we have beans for supper?"

"Go!"

The smell arrives.

"Very nice, Matt," I say. I know how hard he has been working on this.

"Good God, Matthew, you're going to choke us," says Mom. "You stay in the house, *we'll* go outside."

We do. We step through the screen door onto the deck. I think of mice. We settle into the deck chairs. Mom crosses her legs. I don't. You can see the driveway from the deck. The truck sits there. Without its front grill, it looks like it's missing its front teeth. A bit like Grandma at mealtime. A bit like Matthew.

"Don't you think she's a little old for you?"

"Who?" I say again, a little more honestly this time.

Mom crosses her arms and tilts her head at me. She makes her mouth into a flat line. She wags her foot.

"Mom, we're just friends," I say.

"Doesn't she have any *other* friends?"

"Of course she does — she just likes it here. She feels comfortable."

"Why?" asks Mom, knowing full well that *she* has done nothing to make her feel that way.

"Jen's a orphan, Mom," answers Matthew, pushing through the screen door. "She told me." He has tied a brass ring to his left ear and two to his right. He looks like a small, deranged rock star. "Do you like my earrings?" he asks.

+++

I take Matthew and Jennifer for a ride in my truck. *My truck.* I have a truck — an apple green '52 Chevy. I'm calling it "Mac". I'm grinding gears because I'm not comfortable with the ancient stick shift and mechanical clutch. This truck is so old, it doesn't have seat belts. I'm wondering what happens if the cops stop us. What'll they say about a ten-year old with rings tied to his ears?

"Can we go to my place? I want to pick up some stuff," says Jennifer.

"Sure," I say. "Where do you live?"

"By the Dairy Queen, on 8th Street," says Matthew.

"By the Dairy Queen," nods Jennifer.

It doesn't surprise me that Matthew knows this. He seems to know everything. I have never been to Jennifer's place because she not only *has* a boyfriend, she lives with him. She directs me to a nondescript apartment block. We climb the stairs to the third floor. Jennifer searches her purse for keys.

"I hope he's not home," she says.

"Why?" I ask, suddenly nervous.

"He can get pretty weird sometimes."

Jennifer does not get the key all the way into the lock, when the door opens. The door frame is filled with a large man, an *old* man. He has a beard and bare feet.

"Where the hell have you been?" he growls.

"Gerry, this is Matthew," she says, ignoring the question. Her hand is on Matthew's head, "and this is Jesse," she nods to me.

"What are you dragging kids here for?"

"I came for my stuff," she says.

There is a pause, while everyone soaks up what she has said.

"She came for her stuff," says Matthew. His earrings jingle.

Gerry looks at him. A kind of half sneer forms in the middle of his beard.

"Is he retarded? You're hanging out with retards?"

"Nobody's retarded," says Jennifer.

"You, you're retarded," Gerry sneers.

"No, *you're* a retard," bleats Matthew.

Gerry raises his hand to strike Matthew; Matthew ducks, cringing. I jump between them. He hits me instead, on the side of the head. All this takes less than a tenth of a second. He hits me again, for good measure I suppose, this time on the nose. Everything goes black.

When the lights come back on, the first thing I'm aware of is that Gerry's presence is no longer a factor. I'm somehow inside the apartment and Jennifer is half dabbing, half pinching at my nose with a washcloth.

"It's bleeding," she says.

"I'm fine," I say.

"I think it's broken," says Matthew.

"I'm fine," I say again. I try to rise onto an elbow. I'm not fine. I lie back down. "Where's Gerry?"

"I called 911," says Matthew, "and he taked off."

"Yeah, he took off after he hit you. He was scared," says Jennifer.

"Except I dialed the wrong number. I was pretty nervous."

"This is filthy," says Jennifer. She discards the cloth and reaches for her purse. She pulls out what I think is a kleenex. She applies it to my face.

Matthew looks at my nose.

"What is that?" he asks.

"A panty liner," she says.

"A what?"

"Never mind," says Jennifer. "It's superabsorbent," she says to me.

✦✦✦

Jennifer's "things" are pretty meagre: a vinyl suitcase, six or seven small boxes and a large, beat up leather portfolio case. "My art work," she says.

"Where will we take this?" I ask.

"To John's, I guess," she says.

"Who's John?"

"Your Uncle John," she says.

Matthew and I exchange glances. We didn't know they were on a first name basis.

"He said I could store it in the old horse barn."

When we get to the farm, Uncle John's pickup is there, but he's nowhere to be seen. We park Jennifer's boxes in the barn, then head to the house. Inside the back porch sits a gleaming pile of chrome — a new front grill — the last of the body parts.

"Uncle John," Matthew calls. "Hey, Uncle John! You got company!"

There's no answer, but the door to the basement is open and from its depths comes a sound of shuffling. We go to the door.

"Don't come down here," Uncle John says. His voice sounds strange, choked.

Of course, we all go downstairs. And there, sitting on the bottom step, is Uncle John. He's sobbing like a baby.

"What's the matter, Uncle John?" asks Matthew.

Beside the stairs, set tidily against the wall, are an automatic washer and dryer. A large bundle of clothes sits on top of the washing machine.

"I don't know how to work it," sobs Uncle John.

Jennifer places her hand on Uncle John's head. "I'll show you," she says. And she does — she shows him how to work the washing machine. Uncle John thanks her.

Then he kisses her. She welcomes him. The kiss is long. It involves every inch of both their bodies. It's unabashed and unashamed.

I pull Matthew up the stairs.

"Cool," says Matthew.

I nod.

Jennifer doesn't come home with us.

Two weeks have passed. She's still there.

I've installed the new front grill.

I've taken Matthew to get his ear pierced.

I've called Shawna. I've asked her to breakfast. I'll break eggs and fix them scrambled for her. I'll kiss her. I'll let my body go and hope she takes it.

THE CRYING JESUS

The little scar above my lip has been there for six years. I tell people it's from playing hockey. But really, I got it from my sister, Alisa, when I was not yet twelve. Trust her luck that I sport a permanent engraving of the only time she ever hit me — probably the only time she ever sinned. She was thirteen.

Now she is a nun.

My sister the Sister took her vows today, three of them: Poverty, Obedience and Chastity. She lined up in front of the altar with two other novices dressed in white and married Jesus Christ. He was there in spirit. She even got a ring to prove it.

Before she left for the *novitiate*, she gave me her favourite holy picture. It's of the Shroud of Turin, a close-up of the face. The impression, and it is literally that — in dried blood — is no doubt that of a dead man who does not want to talk about it. The only question is whether or not it actually is Christ. My sister, of course, believes it is. Who am I to argue? I'm such a sinner.

It's after the ceremony and she's been allowed to meet with my parents and me in a small reception room. She's radiant. She looks beatified. My mother is crying. She is hugging Alisa. The tears are, I think, tears of joy. Dad looks slightly embarrassed. Tears make him awkward — it doesn't matter what kind they are. Alisa withdraws from Mom's arms then turns to me. She approaches offering her hand. I take it thinking she wants to shake mine but she leads me to a far corner of the room, away from Mom and Dad. We stand beside a small rubber tree. I wonder if it's real.

"Lucas, will you forgive me?" she asks.

Tough question. If I forgive her, I'll be doing God's job.

I dig my thumbnail into the plant's leaf. It bleeds green blood.

◆◆◆

There are two kinds of chastity: there is Chastity, the vow, the kind my sister the Sister took, and Chastity, the girl in my biology class. For two years I've had trouble with both: I ignore one and lust for the other.

Chastity, the girl in my biology class, my lab partner, will break your arm if you call her by her Christian name. Most call her *Chaz*, although some have other names for her. Her parents must have had a wicked sense of humour when they christened her. Either that or she's getting back at them for giving her such a stupid name because Chastity is anything but chaste: she draws lewd pictures — cartoons really — of the football team, as well as of Mr. Bates.

Mr. Bates is our biology teacher. Naturally we call him Master Bates: not to his face, of course, but we think our name for him is very clever and funny. And it is, in a sick sort of way, because he actually is our tour guide into the mysterious world of sex. Except when he talks about it, it's not a very sexy world.

Mr. Bates' classroom sex tours meander through textbook cut-away pictures of body parts erotic as the meat counter at the Co-op. So are the close-ups of tadpole-like things which are somehow the male half of a human being. I don't quite get it. It *is* mysterious.

Chaz's drawings are not. They are graphically potent. For all the mystery of Master Bates' tours, I do know the essentials. But I don't know enough. I don't know how to talk about it because in my church sex is a sin unless you are married and having it to make babies. You are not even supposed to think about it. I think about it anyway, especially when I'm alone in the shower. Or in bed, face down, wads of kleenex strewn about.

I cannot help thinking about it and it is somehow, mysteriously, attached to Chaz. I think about it all the time. I don't think about anything else. In fact, I can't remember what I used to think about before I started thinking about it. All of which leads to what happens in the shower, or in bed, for which I'm going directly to hell.

Is my family religious? Is the Pope? Does a bear shit in the woods? My father dresses in a black cape with red satin lining and goes to Knights of Columbus meetings with a sword. I have no idea what goes on there. Something to do with "defending the faith", presumably of people like my mother who recently chained herself to the step rail of an abortion clinic till firemen came and cut her loose. She might have to go to jail. I have an uncle who is a priest and an aunt who is a nun — not to mention my sister, of course, who is a saint.

Then there's me and Horace. I'm not an out-and-out atheist — I haven't made up my mind yet — but Horace certainly is.

Horace is the family cat.

We have had Horace for seven years. Apparently lost, he followed me home from school one day. I put up signs around the neighbourhood, advertised in the community paper and even called the SPCA, but no one claimed him.

I named him Horace because he looked like one — pompous, sleek, in a shiny black suit, with a ruffled white shirt and tie. I liked him because he was a heathen and got away with it. Nobody said a word when he slept in on Sundays. Nobody questioned his morals. Nobody said boo. Even when he got pregnant.

He was a She.

Those were in the days before I thought about sex all the time because I think that now I would notice Horace was missing the most vital equipment necessary to be a guy — a set of gonads. I don't mind that Horace is a heathen and I don't even mind that he is a she, but it bothers me deeply that she had a litter of kittens before she was spayed.

I also don't mind that my sister is a saint, but saints can be hard to talk to, especially about religion.

"If Christ was God, how come he didn't climb down from the cross and say he had enough?" I ask.

"Because He had to die for our sins," she says. "'And God so loved the world that He gave his only begotten Son.'"

"You don't even know what begotten means."

"I do so," she insists.

"What does it mean then, Alisa?"

"I'll pray for you," she answers.

"Why?"

"Because I'm afraid you're going to hell."

"Why am I going to hell?"

"Your bed squeaks," she says.

She knows. Our rooms are next to each other. She can hear me. There is no point in a long dialectical discussion about recent papal encyclicals in which hell is apparently no longer filled with fire and brimstone, in fact, is no longer even a place, because I'm going there anyway. Whether or not it exists is irrelevant to her.

"Do me a favour please," I ask.

"What?"

"Don't pray for me."

This stops her. She knows I mean it. She also knows that deep down, I like her — that I'm not saying this simply to cause her grief.

"Why not? I *want* to pray for you," she says.

"I want to make it on my own," I say. "It won't count if you help."

She looks at me, warily. "I'll try not," she says.

She will pray for me anyway — secretly, automatically; she won't be able to help it.

So, if you can't talk to your sister without going to hell, who can you talk to? I mean, besides your cat. No one. Certainly not your biology teacher. Perhaps you think about Chaz. You take another lonely shower and spill tadpoles down the drain. You know the guilt of that small shuddering pleasure.

You do not know about the picture, *the Shroud of Turin*.

Thinking about sex all the time and going to hell for it is one thing, but to be constantly reminded of it, twenty-four hours a day, *by a picture*, is something else.

Now the picture has started crying. There are actual tears or some kind of wet stuff oozing through the picture's eyes. Everybody thinks it's a miracle. Maybe it is, but I know why he is crying: Jesus is crying because I am masturbating in the shower. I can't stop.

I have returned the picture to Alisa's room.

✦✦✦

When I say my sister is a saint, I mean it. She was before she became a nun, in fact for as long as I can remember. She is truly holy. Nuns and priests — who are not my relatives — visited her. They prayed together in the basement where Dad built a grotto of the Virgin Mary surrounded by devotion candles. She even got a letter from the Vatican. I don't know what it said.

She wore long-sleeved sweaters and skirts as though she was trying to hide something — like scars, or the *stigmata*, or the mere fact that she has a body.

I must also say this about my sister: she is beautiful. Very beautiful. She has sky-blue eyes that have a way of looking at you, and then beyond — as if she is seeing a better version of you somewhere else. Her smile is quick but seems to linger even after it's actually gone. There is something really delicate, *translucent* about her — like she herself is a sort of temporary vision, a hologram that could vanish at the flick of some cosmic switch. She was probably the most beautiful girl at school. But no one ever asked her out.

It occurs to me that no one ever asks Chaz out either — at least no one that I know of — and it certainly is not because she's a saint, although she too is beautiful. However, unlike Alisa, Chaz has a body that she makes no attempt to hide. I don't mean that she exposes naked flesh for all the world to see, but that she is really comfortable in her skin, a skin, by the way, you want to touch or rub up against. She is a year or so older than the rest of us. She is an athlete in every sport at school except wrestling which is why the jocks call her *Lezbo*, when really, she is simply unattainable. I would love to ask her out. Her body lives in every corner of my mind.

Chaz not only draws lewd pictures of Mr. Bates, with talent and precision, she is equally accomplished at depicting the details of protozoa and all manner of single and multi-celled structures. She can dissect a frog and make slides to count the E. coli in a drop of water. In short, she is a fabulous lab partner. I might even pass because of her. Which is only fair since I might flunk because of her too.

However, I have a plan and I want to include Chaz; I *need* to include Chaz. She knows how to make a slide to slip under a microscope and analyse what's there. I want to see

if Jesus is really crying. I want to test the wet stuff that seems
to be flowing from the picture's eyes.

We are sitting beside each other in class. Mr. Bates is
droning on about lichens. Despite the fact that I see her
almost every day, I'm always amazed at how tall Chaz is, the
length of her legs. It is a constant and torturous surprise.
Chaz's blond hair is cut bluntly about her head and ennun-
ciates the bareness of her gaze. Her mouth, her neck . . .

Never mind, I tell myself, *ask her about making slides of tears.*
I lean over and whisper into her ear.

"Do you want to go out?" I hear myself say.

It's the most astonishing thing. How did my mouth say
those words?

Chaz looks at me, eyes wide. She breaks into great peals
of laughter. A belly laugh. She can't stop. The whole class
is looking at us, wondering what the hell is going on.

"I'm sorry," she says, "I'm sorry," and then breaks into
another fit of laughter. Master Bates is not amused.

"What's going on?" he asks. He strolls up to our desk.
Chaz slaps her hand over a piece of paper upon which she
has been absent-mindedly doodling.

"Can I see that?" he asks.

Slowly she slides her hand down the paper, revealing
millimetre by millimetre the erect proboscis of Mr. Bates'
loins.

Mr. Bates smiles with the corner of his eyes. "Put it away,
Chaz," he says to her and strolls again to the front of the
class. He continues his lichens lecture.

Something has happened here but I have no idea what.

After class, Chaz chases after me. I'm literally rushing for
some place to hide.

"Luc, really. I am sorry."

I can tell from the tone of her voice she means it. I stop.
I look at her. The moment in class that made her laugh so

hard — whatever it was — crosses her mind again. She is fighting back a smile.

"You're so sweet, Luc. You're such a doink. Don't you know?"

"Know what?"

"Luc, I like you — I like you a lot. But . . . ," she hesitates. Her eyebrows furrow into a curious frown. "Can we go for coffee?"

"When?"

"Right now."

"Is this a date?"

"No," she answers too quickly. Then reconsiders, "Well maybe, I don't know. Does it matter?"

"Not really."

"Okay, it's a date."

I'll take whatever I can get.

We are sitting in Taco Time, hunched over coffee. Chastity is nervous. I'm nervous about her being nervous.

"Luc," she says, "I like you."

"Yeah?" I have a feeling there is more.

"I don't want you to take this the wrong way, it's just that I don't like *boys*. I mean I like them, some of them, like you — I'm just not attracted to them."

I suppose my mouth is hanging open now because she adds, "I like *girls*, Luc."

"Oh," I say.

She takes my hand. She smiles. The tension eases. "If I ever want a sperm donor, you'll be on the top of my list."

"Yeah, well, I got lots," I say.

She says she means it. That she loves kids — how she knows her life will not be measured in picket fences, like her mother's, but in some other way, a way she can't yet see.

In this moment, I feel a great sorrow for her but realize it's probably for myself because it strikes me as a great pity that this beautiful woman whom I love, will never be more than a friend — never a lover.

But there is suddenly a great relief in knowing all this. We have just slipped into another gear. I tell her all about thinking about sex all the time, spilling all those tadpoles, and touching the tears on the crying Jesus.

Chaz nods as if she understands. She begins to list the ninety-four minerals and chemicals and their related compounds that compose the essence of tears.

✦✦✦

Horace was getting anxious. She was looking for a place to nest — to have her kittens. I watched her prowl the house and test all the nooks and crannies. She settled for a quiet shelf in Alisa's closet, a place where she kept her sweaters.

Alisa was thrilled about this. She would witness the "miracle of birth". She would rejoice at the blind, mewing "gifts from God". She would rejoice and I would clean up the afterbirth. I always got stuck doing the dirty work — not that I really minded. It never occurred to me that it should be otherwise: an advance *penance*, of a sort, for all my sins.

Horace had eight kittens. Everyone was excited when they were born. But their eyes never opened. They festered instead, like the picture in Alisa's room. Festered till their tiny dark sockets were blind empty holes.

"It's God's will," said Alisa. "Put them in a bag. We will give them back to God."

"How?"

"Just put them in."

I did.

When we got to the river, Alisa put a big rock in the bag with the mewing kittens. She did not tie the bag. We went onto the bridge, to its centre. I flung the bag over the rail.

When it hit the water below, the bag and rock went straight to the bottom. But one by one, all eight kittens rose to the surface in a kind of cluster. They swam in different directions, spreading apart in the great wash of current.

It would have been stupid and useless to try and save them then, though that's what I wanted to do. Alisa stood like a statue and stared where they had been carried downstream and vanished. Maybe she could see their little kitty souls floating up to heaven.

"I hope you're happy," I said. "I hope God's happy too."

She turned, took a full swing and caught me just above the lip.

I bled like a stuck pig.

◆◆◆

I rub the moisture from the leaf between my thumb and forefinger and wonder if rubber really is made from this. My sister the Sister is still waiting for me to answer. She rephrases the question.

"Did I ever ask forgiveness for giving you that scar?"

"You apologized." She apologized a hundred times.

"But did I ask forgiveness?"

"I don't know."

"Will you forgive me?"

"Now?"

"Yes, for what I did to you."

"Jeez, Alisa, it happened years ago."

"I know, but it's important to me."

"Why?"

"It just is."

It dawns on me that I hold the singular key to my sister's happiness. That if I forgive her, she will have a peaceful, saintly life; if I do not, she will be as guilt ridden as the rest of us — with the possible exception of Horace. Life isn't fair. I decide to lie my ass off.

"Of course I forgive you."

"Thank you Lucas," she says to me. She turns to leave. I stop her.

"You know what Chaz and I did?"

"No, what?" There is an ever-so-slight tinge of impatience to the tone of Alisa's voice.

"We analysed the tears in biology class."

Her eyes narrow. She frowns and looks at the rubber plant next to us. She knows I'm talking about the Crying Jesus.

"They were real," I say.

She looks at me and smiles.

"I promise not to pray for you," she says.

MONA WITH THE WHITE LIPS

I would be painting the deck but it's raining. You can't paint in the rain. You can't do much of anything in the rain, unless you're a duck. Or a loon. Right now there's two of them patrolling the dock. I wish I were a loon.

The last person to paint the deck was Uncle Gerry. It was about five years ago, when I was twelve.

Uncle Gerry has a nose like a red running shoe. The bags beneath his eyes hang like the laces are loose. If he doesn't pull himself together, and there's no sign that he will, he's going to fall apart till all that's left are two rows of teeth. They are perfect, though: white-capped and even. Uncle Gerry is a dentist.

He made a fortune mining for gold in people's mouths, then invested in slum apartment buildings. Except that he got into some kind of tax trouble and had to sell them, along with his Porsche, his condo in Phoenix and almost everything else that wasn't nailed down. He was lucky he didn't go to jail. All he has left is a dentist chair, a handful of tools and a mouthful of teeth mingled with inexhaustible bad breath. I used to think he gargled some kind of vile mouthwash. But now I know he just drinks a lot, *like a fish*, as Grandma would say. I think that's why Aunt Mona moved out.

Aunt Mona with the white lips.

She doesn't have white lips now; she *used* to have white lips.

Still waters run deep, says Grandma. She's trying to be nice about Aunt Mona, trying to explain the fact she doesn't talk much, that there's something intense and mysterious about her. However, I have my doubts. Maybe still waters *do* run deep. But still waters also run extremely shallow. Take your average puddle for instance — not too deep but very still. The truth is that Aunt Mona drinks like a fish too. Gin from a teacup.

She and Uncle Gerry never had kids. It's a good thing too. They were extremely awkward around me and my brothers when we were small. They would smile those get-me-out-of-here smiles and hold their drinks a little higher in the air.

Aunt Mona has gone to seed. She spills out of herself like an over-ripe tomato. The shape is still there, but she's gone all soft. She wasn't always like this. Grandma has a picture of her fixed in an old photo album dating back to the sixties. Aunt Mona sits on a stool wearing a very short skirt and long white boots. The skirt and boots do not meet in the middle. They expose elegant thighs. She has a mountain of red lava hair, and holds a cigarette at two o'clock beside her ear. She wears black make-up around her eyes that, opposite her white lips, make her face look top heavy.

However, it's the white lips that get you and it's not as though she's utterly anemic — she has painted her lips white. It is deliberate. The effect is alien, as though she has come for a visit to the planet earth for awhile but can't decide whether she likes it or not. She is edging towards "not".

If anyone is ever coming to take Aunt Mona away (and I'm thinking in terms of spaceships here) I wish they would come now because I'm stuck here alone with her at the lake. I stayed to earn some money by painting the deck. But what is it doing? It's raining. Why is Aunt Mona here? I have no idea. Maybe she has no place to live. She is sitting on the verandah now, reading an old *New Yorker* magazine and fending off mosquitoes. The magazine, like everything else at the cottage, is at least ten years old but Aunt Mona doesn't seem to notice. Just like she doesn't seem to notice the careless way she has left the top three buttons on her blouse undone, or the length of her legs, half-draped with an afghan. She doesn't seem to notice the rain or the wind either. She seems impervious to the cool damp.

Our cottage is in northern Saskatchewan, on an island in a large lake. The big attraction is the view. It truly is spectacular, blue on blue, except when evening shades hit the back of the woods, then it's a sky-full of painted fire. The view and the quiet — so quiet you can hear the whoosh of an eagle's wings a quarter of a kilometre away and the splash as it strikes the water to rise again with a pike locked in its talons. The cottage has been as much a part of the family as Christmas — with the same kind of inevitability about it too, so that even if you don't make it here in a particular year, you miss it. The only problem is getting here, especially when the wind is blowing, something it's doing right now.

It's evening and Aunt Mona has just refilled her teacup with gin. Why the teacup, I don't know. It's not that she's hiding anything or even trying to — the half-full (or half-empty) bottle is on the floor beside the couch. That's what she does — gin from a teacup.

I am trying to build a fire in the wood stove to get rid of the chill. I'm getting soot all over the back of my hand. The matches keep going out. She suddenly lets the magazine collapse on her lap.

"Before I met Gerry," she says to no one in particular, except that I'm the only one around, "I was pretty messed up. I got to thank him for that."

"Huh?" She's made a leap I haven't quite followed; thank him for what?

"He was different then. Of course, we all were different then," she continues. "Did you know I used to be a nun?" she asks me point blank.

"No, I didn't." I think of that picture of her with the white lips. Was that before or after she was a nun?

"I lasted two months," she says laughing. "I wasn't too good at it."

The smoke from the fire I'm trying to light is curling above the stove and settling across the ceiling like an upside down fog.

"What are you doing?" she asks, rising. The afghan falls to the floor.

"Trying to get this going," I say, as if it isn't obvious.

"Let me," she says, padding tentatively across the floor in her white bare feet. I can't imagine them cloistered in black shoes. Her knees crack as she squats next to me in front of the stove. Just for a second she loses her balance and reaches for my thigh to steady herself. The contact is so brief, so accidental and incidental that it's not worth noticing. But I do notice and I'm astonished and embarrassed by the way in which I notice it.

She pokes and prods at the smoke for a moment or two then tells me to open the damper. I do and in a whoosh, the flames burst angry orange. "Fires always remind me of Christmas," she says. "They're so warm."

"Yeah," I say. Fires do not remind me of Christmas. They remind me of wieners.

"We should light the lamps too. It's getting dark."

It's true. It is, and it's only four in the afternoon. You can't tell where the sky starts and the lake ends but its water lashes up against the shore like some stupid black dog at the end of its leash.

"How old are you?" she asks, turning to me suddenly, her face softly awash in the glow of the kerosene lamp.

I tell her but she should know the answer to this. She bought me a set of Oakley driving glasses last year for my sixteenth birthday, anticipating the driver's licence I have not yet got. I wrecked my dad's car practising. He hasn't seen fit to let me practise on his new one. I take the bus.

"That's too bad," she says, settling back onto the verandah couch. "I was going to offer you a drink. I thought you were old enough."

I am old enough. I'm just not old enough to do it legally — is what I think. But not what I say.

"You shouldn't drink so much," is what I say.

"I beg your pardon?"

"I said you shouldn't drink so much."

"You're right, I shouldn't."

"It's not good for you," I insist.

"No, it isn't," she agrees. Then takes a sip from her cup and wipes her lips with the back of her thumb. She smiles and says, "Why do you suppose I do it?"

I'm not sure if this is a real question or if she's asking this just to show me how young and stupid I am, to show me that I'm too young to know the answer to a question like this or even to think of asking such a question. Anyway, it annoys me because I'm not an idiot and she's trying to make me feel like one. I am also annoyed that no one is around to distract her from me right now, that Mom and Dad have gone to town for a doctor's appointment, and they might not make it back because of the weather. I like it better when she's quiet, when she doesn't talk. But she's certainly talking now.

"I'll tell you why," she says, "if you want to know."

I really don't want to know. I really don't care.

"I'm hiding," she says.

Yeah, I think, *I wish you were out of sight.* If she's looking for sympathy, she sure isn't going to find it here. Not only does her pain seem fake, it seems very convenient too, an excuse to drink.

"How come you didn't make it as a nun?" I ask.

"Oh, that's easy — no boys," she says. "I missed them boys you know, especially Gerry. He was pretty cute back then, before he turned into a thief and wife beater."

This shakes me. I had no idea. And that she should say it so nonchalantly. Uncle Gerry, the dentist with a red nose, hits this woman. He hurts my aunt. In my mind's eye I see Uncle Gerry's fist cocked beside his twisted red face. The image loosens something in me. I'm not sure if it's anger or terror. I want to know where he hits her. On the face? Does he leave marks?

"Do you have a girlfriend?" she asks me.

"No, well, yeah, I suppose I do." She's not really a girl-friend — I just go out with her.

"What's her name?"

"Karen, but I don't see much of her."

"That's a nice name. Karen. I knew a Karen once. She used to work at Eaton's."

"Karen doesn't work at Eaton's."

"No, this was years ago. She worked in cosmetics. She sold me lipstick." Aunt Mona laughs. It's a free, clear-stream laugh.

I am immediately transported to grandma's white-lipped photograph. The black make-up around her eyes.

"*White lipstick,*" she says, and laughs some more. I fail to see the humour here. When she stops laughing, she continues. "We wore white lipstick in those days," she says as though she can't believe it. "I wonder why?" She's not asking me. She's asking herself or somebody else in the room who's invisible. "I think we wanted to be English. Those English girls wore it — *Twiggy* — hiding behind those thin white lips. As though we could make ourselves invisible." She takes another drink. "So what are *you* hiding from?"

"Nothing."

"No?"

"No." I'm growing increasingly uncomfortable.

"I think you're hiding from me," she says.

I realize that she is absolutely right, of course. Except that here, in this place, there is really nowhere to hide.

"Am I babbling? I'm babbling, aren't I," she says. "I'll shut up and leave you alone."

She does leave me alone. She disappears back into her magazine and gin while I poke and prod at the fire to keep it ablaze. As the cottage warms and the last rays of the dismal sun are eaten by the cold grey clouds, Aunt Mona falls asleep on the couch.

Or passes out.

Beside her, on the floor, the near empty bottle of gin stands alone. It does, however, have a full friend in the cupboard.

I take both bottles, the full and the near empty, and I go out into the blowing night rain and place them beneath the partially painted deck. I hurry back into the cottage and get ready for bed. No one will be returning tonight. The wind is too high.

The lamp beside Aunt Mona, the verandah lamp, needs to be extinguished along with the others in the cottage. I blow them all out except for a small one I will take with me to the loft. I leave the verandah lamp for last, hoping that Aunt Mona will awake and perhaps put it out herself. But I have the feeling she is gone for the night.

I rearrange the afghan about her and I lean over her, awkwardly reaching for the lamp. My face is inches from hers. She stirs. I freeze. Her eyes actually open for a fraction of a second, then close again.

I pause now and relax into studying her face. Up close, it's surprising, like the moon through a telescope. You can't believe all the texture and terrain — the nooks and crannies, the tiny moles, the bleached hairs above her lip, the slight irregularity at the bridge of the nose, the minuscule broken veins, the little ravines around her eyes. And the scars.

The scars are high on her right cheekbone and in both her eyebrows. They are extremely fine. Someone has done a very good sewing job — *suturing* job. But I know now where Uncle Gerry hits. Even in the yellow of the lamplight the vague, almost imperceptible raise of the suture seam glints in contrast with the rest of Aunt Mona's bloodless pallor — her lips especially. For the briefest moment I think of what it might be like to kiss those lips. I raise the lamp chimney and blow out the flame. I go to bed.

◆◆◆

Somewhere in the middle of the night, I awaken. It's not from any discernible sound, or even the opposite — a sudden quiet. It's from the powerful feeling that I'm being watched. The storm has passed and the moon is careening crazy light around the cottage. There is a silver-framed silhouette in the doorway.

It's Aunt Mona, still in her shorts and blouse.

"Gerry?" she calls.

"What?" I answer. I'm sleep-stupid. I know I'm not Gerry but I can't think of what else to say.

"What did you do with it?"

"What?" This time I'm confused. And, she is approaching.

"Did you drink it?"

"I'm not Gerry," I say. "And no," I add, "I didn't drink it."

"Where did you hide it, Gerry?"

"It's me, Aunt Mona, Kevin."

"Where's Gerry?" she asks.

"He's not here, Aunt Mona. You don't live together."

"Did you hide it, Kevin?"

"Hide what?"

"My gin," she says.

"No," I lie.

Aunt Mona gathers herself into some approximation of the here and now. "Kevin, I seem to have misplaced my gin. Would you help me find it?"

"Now?"

"Please," she insists, "now."

"Okay." I can't disagree. I sit up and reach for the matches lying beside the lamp. I scuff one against the pack. In the sudden flare I realize I am only wearing a pair of white cotton briefs. But it's already too late. I'm locked in her eyes while stretching to raise the thin glass chimney — lighting the lamp.

Settling the chimney back into place, I glance up at her. She has the merest hint of a smile on her lips. I pull the covers over my lap. She turns away when I grab my jeans hanging over the back of a chair.

"Sorry," she says. It doesn't matter if she means it or not.

❖❖❖

We have now finished searching the cottage. We are seated on the couch in the verandah.

"There was a bottle right there," she indicates the floor beside the couch, "I'm sure I left it there. And one in the cupboard. And now they're gone."

Why I'm pretending that this is some great mystery is an equally great mystery to me. Why am I doing this?

"Did Gerry come in here and take them?" she asks.

"There's no one on the island but us."

"Well, if it wasn't Gerry and it wasn't me, then it must have been you."

"Why would I do that?"

"I don't know. Why did you?"

"You shouldn't drink," I say

"So you keep reminding me." She looks at me frankly, challenging. "Did you break the bottles?"

"No," I say.

"Ah, good," she says and smiles. "What do I have to do to get them back?"

Now this is interesting. I'm suddenly in a position of power. I can name my terms. What do I want? As I'm thinking of the possibilities, it occurs to me this isn't the question at all. The question is, *do I want anything?* And I know the answer — *not really.* I'd be happier if daylight came and my parents were here so none of this would have happened. Or that none of what might happen, will happen.

"What *can* you do?" I ask.

"I can do anything," says Aunt Mona. "There are certain things I *won't* do — but I *can* do anything."

"What won't you do?" I ask.

Aunt Mona laughs. "Oh, hardball, eh?" she says. She clears her throat and straightens herself on the couch. "Between you and me Kevin, there isn't anything I wouldn't do."

This isn't hardball — it's tennis. The ball is suddenly back in my court. Aunt Mona has the advantage.

You wouldn't kill me, would you? I think, and the thought must somehow register on my face because she answers.

"I might."

"For a bottle of gin?"

"It *would* be silly, wouldn't it? I mean, you'd be dead. How would I get my gin? I could *threaten* to kill you. I could hold a gun to your head." She looks about the room as though to see if there's one handy. "Or a knife to your throat — but that would be just so . . . *dumb*. No, I don't think I would need to be violent. I could probably just embarrass you to death."

"How?"

"Do you really want to know?"

I shrug my shoulders.

She unbuttons the fourth button on her blouse.

I go get the bottles.

✦✦✦

The lake is quiet and calm, that post-storm steely calm — the kind that hints of fall. It would be utterly barren if it weren't for the loons. They're still on patrol. Although they can hear it, it's not until the boat rounds the point, and I can recognise Grandma with my parents, that one of the loons takes flight above the waves while the other dives beneath.

Aunt Mona saunters down towards the dock while we are unpacking the boat. She wears a pair of jeans with the pant legs rolled above her ankles and a loose sweater. As she approaches, her smile takes us all in and I feel a pang of guilt although I know I've done nothing wrong.

She and Grandma greet. They hug. Aunt Mona holds Grandma's hand and helps her to the cottage. Together they admire the new coat of paint on the deck. They agree that if the job had been done right first, it wouldn't need redoing now. They don't mention Uncle Gerry.

CURSING SHANE

There are cultures where monkey eyeballs are a delicacy. I don't know if they cook them first or eat them raw. But the thought of those gristly orbs popping their juice onto your tongue as you grind your jaw is not one that appeals at all. However, I would like to gouge Shane's eyeballs with the hooks of my thumbs and stick them in his mouth. It would fill me with satisfaction to see him quiver as they exploded between his teeth.

Really, would that be so wrong?

I write these things in my diary. To keep track of how I feel. I keep it in my purse.

But truly, he stalks me. He watches. He calls me on the phone. Sometimes he doesn't speak, but I know it is him. He buys me gifts.

"I love you," he says. "I can't live without you."

"Try," I say.

"Why won't you see me?"

"You have bad breath," I say. This isn't the truth but he's so vain that he'll now spend a fortune gargling bottles of mouth rinse. Perhaps he'll drink some and go blind.

"My breath is fine," he says. "It's you."

He's right. It *is* me. I want nothing to do with him.

"Get lost," I say. I walk away.

He follows.

I've considered placing a curse on him but I believe too much in their power and know too little of their meaning. It's the preferred weapon of the powerless: guns are loud; knives are sharp; poisons are awkward and slow. A curse is silent, deft and mysterious. A curse could kill.

This summer I have a job. My family are devout Catholics and my father has arranged for me to work at the Catholic hospital where he's a senior administrator. The hospital was run by nuns, and although there are only a few of them around now, they are under the impression that I'm soon going to enter the convent, to be one of them. I suppose there was a time when I wanted to be a nun, but not now, not any more. Still I'm grateful for the job. I'll play the little charade. There's no harm. I need the money. I'll be going away to school in a year. It won't be too soon.

One of them, Sr. Fatima, has either taken a liking to me or she has been assigned by someone (my father?) to keep an eye on me. She is an old-fashioned, old nun — still wearing a modified wimple — with the face of a poker player. At any rate, she always seems to show up when I'm near the end of one task in order to lead me seamlessly to the next. "Work is prayer," she tells me, as though this will somehow break the mind-numbing monotony.

I work the evening shift, three to eleven. The job I have is formally called a "Temporary Full-time Replacement Worker", which means I do a little of everything, provided it's menial enough. I will not be replacing any brain surgeons. So, depending on which department is most understaffed because of holidays and budget cuts, I'll work in either the laundry, where I was this week, the kitchen, where I was last week, or in housekeeping, where I'll work next week. I'm looking forward to the change.

When I get off work, Shane is waiting near the staff exit in his car. This was fine when we were going out, but now it isn't. He doesn't leave his car, he simply watches as I cross the street to the bus stop. The street is well lit. I'm not particularly afraid and have timed it so that my bus arrives pretty much as I do. I've thought of asking my father to pick me up but that would be admitting trouble and I don't want him to know.

Shane is nowhere to be seen as I step from the bus to walk the half block to my house, but I know he's there, somewhere. I can *feel* his presence.

The phone often rings as I enter the door.

"I care about you," says Shane.

I hang up.

Last week he called to say he was going to kill himself.

"Go for it," I said.

The next morning, the tires to father's car were slashed.

◆◆◆

Shane leans against his locker picking a victim. He wants to show me his power. "Hey you," he says quietly.

The kid turns, surprised.

"Come here," Shane says.

This is the test. If he comes, Shane knows he has him. If he walks away, no problem, there is always someone else.

Let's say he comes.

"You ever seen one of these?" Shane asks. From his pocket he pulls an oblong metal apparatus made of brass. He slides it over his knuckles. "You know what these are?"

Even if the kid has never seen a set before, he nods in recognition.

"I'll take care of you," Shane says, "just give me ten bucks a week." The kid's face looks like it will crack. "If you don't,

who knows what kind of mess you could have." And Shane
smiles, his beautiful white teeth gleaming like night snow.
"You know what I mean?"

The kid nods again, speechless.

"What's your name?" he asks the kid.

The kid's name is Jeffrey.

"Jeffrey, guess what?"

"What?" Jeffrey manages to ask.

"I'm kidding," says Shane. He looks over at me, his eyes
smiling. "I wouldn't do something like that to you, Jeffrey
— I like you. Do you like me?"

The kid, Jeffrey, is so confused and terrified by now that
his skinny little legs are visibly trembling. He might shit
himself. He nods.

"What? I can't hear you," says Shane.

"Yeah, I do," says Jeffrey.

"You do what?"

"I like you," Jeffrey utters.

"How can you like me, Jeffrey? We hardly know each
other."

"That's enough, Shane," I say.

"I'm just talking to Jeffrey, Cynthia — aren't I, Jeffrey?"

Jeffrey's eyes flicker back and forth between me and
Shane. He's pathetically frozen.

"Leave him alone," I say.

"You can go now, Jeffrey. But Jeffrey," Shane places his
hand on Jeffrey's shoulder, "we'll get to know each other
soon, okay?"

Jeffrey gulps, "Yeah." He's gone.

Shane turns to me. "That's power," says Shane.

✦✦✦

"Who me?" he says with such menacing innocence that any
interrogations stop there — usually. There have been ex-
ceptions, mostly centering around the time he was caught
with a stolen pellet gun and went popping out windows of
teachers he did not like. He spent some time in Wilbur Hall
because his parents could not handle him.

You must know this about Shane: his intimidation doesn't
come from size. He is small and blond. His eyes are a toxic
green. He can fix you with them like you've been shot with
venom — paralyzed. Then he'll slowly drain you dry. This
is what he's done to me.

I first went out with him because I was charmed — by his
smile, his sensuous mouth, his perfect teeth and, of course,
his eyes. Although I have never seen him cry, he says he
does so all the time — for me, when we're apart. I suppose
it could be true, but he's such a perfect liar that there's not
much room for truth.

With Shane, nothing is ever as it seems. His simplest
words have double meanings. His gifts always *mean* something or other: red and white roses for fire and water — a
union of opposites; an *ouroboros* ring — a snake eating its
tail. *My end is my beginning,* says Shane. Where he gets money
to buy these things, I don't know.

He gives me an orange. "The blossom," he says, "sym-
bolizes purity." The orange is laced with vodka. This he cuts
in quarters and shares with me. The juice dribbles down my
chin and throat. He licks me there. We kiss. We kiss. If this
is a movie, the lens blurs, grows dark. The music swells. We
fade to another time and place.

✦✦✦

At the hospital is a Canadian Corps Commissionaire. He's
been there for years — since I can remember, certainly since

my father began working there. He's a fixture; his name is Carl, a gargoyle in a black uniform. There's something about him that makes me uneasy. I don't know what it is. He's pleasant enough. He nods, smiles and takes old people by their arms. But he leers like a cat when he sees me. His teeth are sharp and pointy. He too works the evening shift.

◆◆◆

Today at work, Sr. Fatima calls me over.

"Cynthia, you are studying to see God; then you must see death." She takes me to a room near emergency. It is small, white, well-lit. In its centre is a table. On it lies a man. He is dead. Sr. Fatima makes the sign of the cross and nods towards him. My knees buckle, but I recover. We stand in silence for a time.

"What are your thoughts?" she asks.

In truth, I have no thoughts. I've been staring at the man. He's a workman in his forties, still wearing his work clothes — green shirt and pants. His feet are splayed apart. On them are well-worn workboots. There is blood, now coagulated, that's leaked from his nose and mouth as well as his ears and eyes. There are bits of clay caked into the blood.

Yet this is not so remarkable.

What is astonishing is the broadness of his shoulders, or what *seems* to be the broadness of his shoulders. This is because his ribs have all been collapsed, upward, like hands folded in prayer.

"My thoughts . . . " I stall. Thoughts are now indeed beginning to form. *If I must see this to see heaven, then what must I see to see hell?* I don't ask this.

"What happened?" I ask.

Sr. Fatima frowns. "The earth fell on him — in an excavation accident," she says flatly.

"He looks heavy," I say, imagining trying to lift him.

"He looked surprised," says Sr. Fatima, "before I closed his eyes."

For a moment I see Shane.

"I suppose we would all have that look — if the earth fell on us," I say.

"If we are not prepared," she says pointedly.

I nod in agreement, although I'm thinking, *How could you be prepared for the earth falling on you?*

Sr. Fatima seems happy now. She ushers me from the room. "Did you know him?" she asks me. The question surprises me. I had never seen him before and I tell her that.

"He was my brother," she says.

I'm not sure I've heard her correctly. I turn sharply to look at her. "Yes," she says. "My baby brother. Pray for his soul, Cynthia." She touches my arm. "He was not blessed, Cynthia. He was cursed." She looks at me for a second, as though she's saying something else. She then walks away.

✦✦✦

"What were you talking about?" Shane asks.

"With who?"

"You know damn well who."

"No, I don't. I can't read your mind."

I do know. I was talking with Kevin after class. He was flaring about how stupid geometry is and wanted me to help him. I said I would.

"If I see you talking to him again, I'll break his face."

"I can talk to whoever I like."

"If I see you *looking* at him, I'll break yours."

"I can look at, talk to, *sleep with* whoever I want."

Shane slaps me in the face. It's so sudden and abrupt that we're both shocked.

"I'm sorry," he says, "I'm sorry. I didn't mean that."

"You hurt me."

"You hurt *me*," he says.

"Go away."

"It was a reflex, I'm sorry."

"Go away. Don't ever touch me again."

"I'm sorry," says Shane.

+++

I have not explained, really, how I'm attracted to Shane, how I love him and how I keep hoping for him to change. I have not explained because I can't; I don't know. I'm like Jeffrey in some ways.

He calls me again.

"You don't know what I go through," he says.

"Spare me."

"You have no idea. You don't know me. You don't know what I have to go through."

"Tell someone who cares," I say.

"I love you," he says.

I hang up.

+++

Today my father has lent me the car to go to work. He'll do this on Saturdays when he and mother have no plans for the evening. I do have plans. I'm meeting Kevin and some friends after work on 8th Street where we hang out and talk. Kevin passed his geometry and wants to buy me a coffee. He says it's the least he can do.

Sr. Fatima wasn't at the hospital today. She was with her
family, having attended her brother's funeral. The shift was
longer than usual — not in real time but simply in the
unbroken drudgery of scrubbing porcelain and tile grout.
I cleaned the room where her "baby brother" had lain. I
could see him in my mind's eye still there. If "work was
prayer" as Sr. Fatima had said, then her brother had died
praying. How could he have been cursed? It occurred to
me that if I was in fact praying, then God was in the sink.

I hurry from the staff room to leave the hospital, and as
usual Shane is parked outside. As usual, he doesn't move.
I cross the parking lot and climb into my father's car. As I
back from the parking space then manoeuvre ahead, I have
the urge to slam the heavy grill of my father's Lincoln into
the low-hanging side of Shane's Camaro. I drive by instead,
planning to give Shane the finger as he watches me pass.
However, he doesn't look at me. His gaze is fixed on something else. I'm suddenly alarmed.

It's about a ten minute drive to where I'm meeting my
friends and by the time I arrive, I've forgotten all about
Shane, God and Sr. Fatima's dead brother.

I've also forgotten my purse.

In my rush to leave the hospital, I remember leaving the
purse on the staff table. I remember first removing my
father's keys from it, then closing my locker. I'm hoping the
purse still sits on the table.

I run into the restaurant to tell my friends of my predica-
ment. They are appropriately concerned. They know about
Shane, that he's likely somewhere around. I'm also hoping
that Kevin will return with me to the hospital. He does.

"What do you know about curses?" I ask him.

"I curse all the time," he says.

"No, I mean real curses," I say.

"Oh, like boil and bubble stuff," he says.

"Yeah."

"I don't know anything," says Kevin. "Why?"

"I want to place one on Shane," I say.

"You're too late. He's already cursed," says Kevin.

We pull into the parking lot. I'm startled to see Shane's car parked in the same place it was earlier. Shane, however, is nowhere to be seen.

"Wait here," I say to Kevin, "I'll be right back."

Kevin nods.

I arrive in the staff room, open the door and am stunned to see Sr. Fatima seated comfortably at the table. She is reading my diary. It looks as though she has dumped the purse's contents on the table. She is clearly rattled by my entrance. She slaps the diary shut and immediately begins stuffing the contents back into the purse.

"What are you doing?" I ask.

"I was checking to see who it belonged to."

"You were checking my diary. Did you find it interesting?"

"Yes, as a matter of fact, I did. Does your father know?" She recovers quickly.

"No. And he'd better not find out."

"I'm sorry for you," she says,

"Don't be."

"You are not going to enter the *novitiate.*" This is not a question. It's a statement of fact.

"No, I'm not."

"Good. I'll pray for your young man. For him *there will be joy in heaven.*"

She is quoting the Bible and implying that as bad as he is, Shane'll get to heaven through the front door, whereas I'll have to sneak in through the back. She hands my purse to me and briskly leaves the room.

How did she do that? I was the one who was wronged, and yet I feel as though I've been hit in the stomach. In a daze, I return down the stairs and out the door towards Kevin in the car.

"You wouldn't believe what happened," I begin.

"Sh-sh," he says, "Look." He points across the parking lot to where an older model car sits in a darker corner. I immediately recognize it as belonging to Carl, the Commissionaire. The dark shape of a head can be seen behind the windshield. "There's a couple in there making out," says Kevin.

"With Carl?" I don't believe it.

"Who's Carl?"

"That's his car. He works here."

"Well there were *two* heads in there a while ago. The other one kind of disappeared — *down*. And then there's this, kind of like, *fidgeting*."

As the words leave his mouth, the second head reappears on the passenger side. There is a brief exchange between them. Then the passenger door opens. A figure emerges. He closes the door and puts something into his pocket. As he begins to walk across the parking lot, the older car slowly pulls away. The drivers face glints in the parking lot light. It *is* Carl.

The figure walking across the parking lot is Shane. He stops under a lamp, reaches into his pocket with his right hand and pulls out something that he places into his left hand. He licks his index finger and begins leafing through whatever is in his left hand.

"What's he doing?" I ask.

"I think he's counting money," says Kevin.

I start my father's car, then turn on the headlights and catch Shane full in the face. His eyes are startled wide. His mouth is open. In that moment I'm filled with remorse.

There is a perfect sadness to people when you catch them in that moment of open blindness, uncovered, clean. Like a first snowfall in its pale grace. A curse is like that. It is surprising.

Eating with the Dead

Although my name is Penny, I have always fit inside my dime-sized self, and ten of me would scarcely crowd a phone booth. But dollar or dime, the currency here — the issue — is not money, it's food.

My mother was corralled into a single large skin. She was obese. Unhealthily so. It was not "glandular" or some other physical disorder, she just ate a lot, despite the fact that she was constantly dieting. She went on all kinds of weight-losing schemes, the most recent involving some combination of bananas and grapefruit. Still, she would end up just a little bit fatter than she was before.

I told her about the incredible, sixteen-day, seal diet.

"Seals?"

"Yes, you eat seals for sixteen days and you lose 40% of your body weight."

She looked at me. She *wanted* to believe me, but she knew I was baiting her.

"You shouldn't," she said to me, "do that."

Inside every fat person there is an even fatter one screaming to get out. The truth is that seals lose about ninety kilos — 40% of their body weight — in around sixteen days. Unfortunately they have to be nursing their young to do it. They deliver four kilos of milk a day, and 60% of the milk is fat. I had seen this in a nature documentary and the stats had stuck.

However, it was the brief, startling image of me nursing from my mother that almost made me gag. Yet I did nurse from her as an infant. She said that's when she started gaining weight — 40% of it. The weight was terribly hard on her heart. She could barely walk across the room.

She had little solace inside our house, or out — she loathed the cold. In a place where it is winter for seven months of the year, this was a problem. Maybe that's why she ate so much — to provide the insulation. It didn't work.

"I hate the cold," she would say.

"Put on your coat," I would say.

"It doesn't fit," she would say.

This, of course, was sadly true. Nothing fit. She lived in baggy things — tents she called them. She hadn't left the house in two years. I would bring her a blanket. She would read her tea.

"I see warmth," she would say.

"Well, that's good, Mom," I would say.

"Unfortunately, it won't arrive till I am dead," she said, smiling. Then looked at me as though I should or could do something about this.

"What?" I asked.

"Get me a banana," she said.

"That won't warm you," I said.

"Get me a banana," she repeated.

My earliest memories focus on food: my fat baby fingers picking at french toast, drowned in maple syrup, dipped in cream; my mother rolling dough, pinching it into rings and dropping them into a bubbling pot of oil — doughnuts, frosted with berry sugar; my father with heaps of liver fried with bacon, slathered in onions. I remember staring at the lone yellow eye of an egg and it staring back at me; the green tugging of split-peas at my gorge. Food is interactive

— and if you are what you eat, then you are also *not* what you avoid eating.

I got her the banana. I handed it to her.

"Eat it," she said, handing it back.

"No," I said.

How could I? — publicly, that is. Privately I gorge then disgorge. I don't think about it. I just do it. Overeating is supposed to be as bad as undereating. Tell that to a mirror. Inside every thin person, there is an even thinner one peering through the rib cage. I weigh forty-one. Kilos.

"Eat it, please," she said again.

"No," I wouldn't.

"Why will you never eat with me?" she asked, in martyr mode.

"Because."

"That's no reason."

"I'm not hungry," I offered.

"Hunger has nothing to do with it," she said, mystically.

"What will you do if I eat the banana?"

"I'll die happy," she said. "I deserve to die happy — I've lived such a miserable life."

This, of course, was also true. She, *we*, had pretty well been abandoned by my father and the only other family we might have had — an uncle who lived in California.

"I'll bury you someplace warm," I said, making a very bad joke and instantly regretting it.

"Good!" she said. "That would make me happy too."

I realized that I might have made a commitment here, one that I wouldn't really want to keep. But I was already thinking of the possibilities.

"Tell my brother he's an asshole," she said. Reading my mind.

It was no great surprise when she died, although I felt somehow responsible, and it was not easy to deal with alone. My father did show up for the funeral. There were tears in his eyes when he hugged me but there was beer on his breath and I couldn't wait for him to leave. Mom weighed over a hundred and eighty kilos — that's four hundred pounds if you're not into metric — and I had her cremated. I couldn't stand the thought of people trying to lug her impossible weight over an early October snow just to put her into a hole. Somebody could slip and get seriously hurt. Besides, I had made her that vague promise. Winter was coming on. There would be no warmth for her — unless I took her to it, to Uncle Keir's.

Uncle Keir lives in California and makes movies. Although I have never met him, I have seen photographs of him as a boy. He is gaunt and dark. He looks like he is about to ask a very clever question that no one can answer — like, "Why should I be here?" The point is he isn't here — hasn't been for years, and didn't come to the funeral. He sent only a sympathy card. So I am going to see him, this uncle of mine, present him with his sister's ashes, and maybe get into the movie business. I have sent him a note to this effect.

"Yes, Penny," he will say, "come down to the studio lot today. Or the office. Or the set of our latest feature film. I'm sure we can find something for you to do." He will speak in the first person, plural. Like the queen and like country stars. "But what will we do with this?" he will ask, looking at my mother in a box. I will tell him. Then I will rest. I will get a California tan. I will forget about my mother. It will make me shiver to think of home.

My mother has appeared to me in bits and drabs, like crumbs after the main course. I took the tiny bit of insurance money, sold everything, and bought a used quarter-ton pickup with a camper on the back. I put Mom in the truck cab beside me — her box of ashes — and hit the road.

✦✦✦

The world seems so enormous when you are travelling alone across endless ranges of land, cruising inches above it, kept aloft by spinning disks of rubber — tires — no one part of them meeting the road for any time longer than the least part of a second. It is as though you exist outside of time, even those moments when you are captured by some magnificent scene — a spread of plain or miraculous fold of mountain. In a way I do exist outside of time — inside it only when I stop for gas or the bathroom. I pull off the road somewhere in Idaho to sleep, and in that sleep, time exists in the same way my tires do when they meet the road at 120 kliks per hour.

The second day, I sweep through Nevada, climb through Reno and descend into the warm bed of California. Even though it is late October the heat still lingers, like some giant has recently risen then moodily departed south, drawing a great clean rake across the valley. Water does not flow free here: it is channeled, focused tight, like the interstate I am rolling on, and like all plant life — groves, orchards, vineyards and fields — all marshalled into strict lines of authority.

I begin to notice the Spanish. It appears more and more the further south I go. It is not only in the signage, but the architecture as well — a more apparent influence here than French in Canada. I tell Mom this. She is silent — relaxed.

I spend the second night in a campground beside the interstate near a town called Bakersfield. The campground is a barren patch of concrete and dirty brown grass amid groves of pistachios. I know the groves are pistachios because a sign in the registration office tells me to visit *Pistachio Pete's*, a *cantina* dedicated to the local crop. I pass on *Pete's*, although Mom would have approved. I go to sleep. I want to make Uncle Keir's tomorrow.

The next morning, it's raining hard. I thought it didn't rain in southern California.

All I have is the return address from Mom's sympathy card. I buy a map of greater L.A. to guide me. Los Angeles is not like you see it in the movies. It is dirtier. And way bigger. Mammoth. It goes on forever. The traffic is as tense as it is intense. I have always been good at maps but this is a labyrinth. I pick my path and despite the fact that I have no idea where I am going, I stick resolutely to my route. Everything is festooned in black and orange. Paper skeletons and pumpkins decorate shop windows. It's Halloween. I'd forgotten.

I'm driving up a mountain. The windshield has sprung a leak. I have this absurd fear that Mom will wash away.

The rain lets up. Visibility improves. I arrive at the address.

It is a palace. It is a mansion spread like the days of a week. A camera, mounted high on a wrought-iron gate, follows me as I drive past it and onto the driveway.

Palm trees and cacti line the driveway. Near the front door is an arrangement of rock and desert plants strung with orange and black crepe paper drenched absurdly in the rain.

I'm greeted at the door by Uncle Keir's spandexed wife, an aunt I have never met. I can't tell if this is the way she normally dresses or if she is preparing to go out trick-or-treating. She tells me to call her Lucy. She is fixing her face with a plastic smile, extending her bejewelled hand and apologizing for Uncle Keir's absence. He is in Mexico making a movie — *Time Bomber*. She invites me in. I enter. She then vanishes, leaving me alone in the foyer.

On a small table is a brass business card holder. In it are my uncle's cards. I take one. It says, *Sunrise Films Inc. Keir Hilfrig, Executive Producer* followed by a Hollywood address and two phone numbers. I slip the card into my bag as Aunt Lucy returns.

I have never been in a house like this before. There are several levels that you would never have guessed existed from the outside, and each of the levels seems to be devoted to a different epoch of human civilization. Above the foyer — to the left — appears to be medieval, judging by the little armoured men with swords standing guard to brass-bound doors. Down and to the right is a *Star Ship* entertainment centre, complete with lasers and a three-dimensional chess set. Straight ahead is a room out of the old west, filled with saddles and rope and gnarled wood. It's to this room that I am being led, past another room with giraffes and palm trees.

I'm seated on a leather couch. It feels like a stuffed dead cow — which it may well be. I smile *my* plastic smile. Aunt Lucy offers me a cup of coffee and informs me that I don't look like she expected me to look.

"Are you anorexic?" she asks.

"No," I say. "I'm thin."

"Oh," she says. "Well we know your mother wasn't."

"She's in the truck," I say — adding, "her ashes."

She goes on to sympathize what a tragedy it was that I had to care for her, and what a shame it was that Uncle Keir couldn't have been there to help. She somehow says all this without moving her lips. They are fixed around her teeth.

She compliments my plaid slacks.

"Is it the family tartan?" She wants to know about my father's family.

I say no, it's not. But I am still stunned by the fact that I am sitting with a stupid strange woman, my Aunt Lucy, who is asking essentially why I don't eat more. I don't know why, and all the while I am thinking this, I am still babbling "no" to the question of the tartan, that even though my great, great grandfather carried his Gaelic pipes to the hills of Cape Breton, and that my great grandfather worked under those hills mining for coal, and that my grandfather moved to the prairies to guard German prisoners of war during World War Two, and that my alcoholic father sells cars and would rather be drinking — that, "no", this is not the family tartan. I don't know what the family tartan is. I am just their daughter, the end of the patriarchy, a conclusion in blood — or sweat — which I feel, by the way, dripping from my freshly shaven armpits.

Aunt Lucy has been sitting there, her head cocked to one side, giving the appearance that she has been listening to me while I have been nailing myself to the family tree. Whether or not she has been listening, I don't know, because she rests her coffee on her plump, spandexed knee and poses for a moment.

"What do you eat?" she asks.

"Eat?"

"Are you on a diet?" She attempts to clarify.

"No," I say, "I've never been on a diet." If I were to go on a diet, it would be in order to add more flesh onto my meagre bones.

"Keir is on a diet," she says.

"Oh?" I say, quizzically.

"Yes," she says, "bananas and grapefruits. That's all he eats."

"That's incredible," I say.

"Why?" she asks.

I tell her about my mother's final diet.

"Bananas and grapefruit," she says.

I look at the clock. It is hanging on the wall above a mantel festooned with ancient western weapons. The face of the clock is set inside the carcass of an armadillo. I think, *mutant clock armadillos.* The time reads four fifteen.

"Hideous, isn't it," Aunt Lucy says, seeing me look at the clock.

"Yes," I agree, marvelling at how the little stuffed armadillo's head seems to be peering down at what used to be its stomach.

"Would you like it?" she asks, rising.

"No." I feel a wave of panic swelling in me and I wish that Uncle Keir would have been here to rescue me from this madwoman, his wife.

"It was a gift from Keir," she says. She is now dragging a stool towards the mantel. "Please, take it." She climbs the stool.

"No, really."

"I want you to have it," she says, and begins to dislodge the dead armadillo.

"I'd have no use for it."

"I insist." She clumps down from the mantel.

"I don't want it."

"Please." She crosses the room.

"No, thank you."

"Take the goddamn armadillo," she says handing it to me as though it were still alive. She is breathing hard — all this exertion. She returns to her chair, sits and takes a deep breath. She then looks at me as though she has something very important to say.

I look at her, expectantly.

She speaks.

"Don't take this personally, Penny, but we don't want anything to do with your family." She pauses here, either to see my reaction or think of something else to say.

The absurdity is too much to bear.

"You *are* my family!" I say.

"Well actually, Penny, we would prefer not."

I suppose I am gawking at her with my mouth open.

She smiles at me as though I have just presented her with a box of rare chocolates. Then she rises and turns towards the door. I know this is a cue. I stumble behind.

When we get to the foyer, she asks if I have my armadillo.

"Yes," I say. The thing is clinging to me. If I had been thinking, I would have just left it on the cow couch.

"It was absolutely fabulous meeting you," Aunt Lucy smiles as she opens the door.

"Thank you," I say. It's a reflex. I certainly don't mean it. I can't believe how polite I'm being. So, for effect, I pitch the armadillo at the doorframe above Aunt Lucy. She jumps. The armadillo bounces between us. One ear breaks off.

"What are you doing?" Aunt Lucy wants to know. Her lips move.

"I don't know," I say.

But I know exactly what I am doing — I am going to track down Uncle Keir.

I phone the offices of *Sunrise Films Inc.*, I ask where *Time Bomber* is being shot. I buy another map. This one is of Mexico.

◆◆◆

I arrive at Pitiquito. Filming has been halted because of the torrential rains. Uncle Keir, I am told, is at his retreat on Isla Tiburon. You can get there in half an hour by helicopter, or a day's drive plus a ferry crossing from Babia Kino.

Parts of the road have vanished. I lose my muffler on a rock I didn't see. I roar on to Babia Kino, passing people with cartloads of flowers. They look at me with undisguised hostility.

Then I run out of gas.

I know I'm somewhere between Hermosillo and Babia Kino. The reason I've run out of gas is because I've been too afraid of stopping to ask for it. I'm embarrassed by my lack of Spanish. I'm embarrassed by the difference I see between myself and those parading in the rain with their

cartloads of flowers pulled by donkeys or broken-down
horses. I am embarrassed and afraid.

One of the carts I passed earlier is approaching. It's being
pulled by a small grey donkey. I grab my purse and the box
with mother in it. I get out of the truck.

A man and a woman with a small child huddle on the
cart beneath a sheet of tattered blue plastic. They stop when
they get to me.

"Gasoline? *Petról?*" I say indicating the truck. They look
at me. The child buries its head into its mother's folds. They
say nothing. "Babia Kino," I say the name of the town.

Suddenly the man jumps down from the cart. He crosses
in front of the donkey.

"*Por favor,*" he says. He tries to take my box from me. I
jerk it back.

"No. No," he says. He backs up and graciously bows,
indicating that I should join them on the cart.

"Thank you, *gracias,*" I say one of the few Spanish words
I know. I climb onto the cart. The woman smiles. She shifts
the child — it is a boy — and carefully makes room for me,
arranging the plastic to shelter us all.

As we approach the town, more carts and trucks and
every manner of vehicle also seem to be converging there.
We plod to the town's centre — a market square — where
preparations are clearly under way for some kind of cele-
bration. There are dozens of stalls all sheltered by canvas
or plastic tarps. They are filled with flowers and grotesque
masks and small ornamental decorations.

"What is this?" I gesture, my palms up. I exaggerate
looking around.

"*Día del Muerto,*" says the mother smiling again. I'm not
sure what she is saying. "The day of something." She is
missing her two front teeth. The little boy smiles now too.
He is missing the same teeth — but his will grow.

"Babia Kino," says the man. He stops the donkey then helps his wife and son to the muddy ground. He indicates that I should get down too. He does not offer to help.

Moments later I'm standing awkwardly in the rain holding my mother's ashes while I watch the three of them systematically unload the cart of orange flowers and quickly build their stall. "Babia Kino," the man says again, throwing his hands above his shoulders. It is now that I realize that I am only a ferry ride from my uncle.

"*Gracias, gracias,*" I say to them and immediately leave to find the ferry.

I wander the market square and examine more closely some of the wares. The decorative ornaments are not really ornaments at all but candies made to resemble skeletons or angels, all laughing and smiling. Women haggle over their worth, then nod curtly and make an exchange of currency for the candy.

Mother's box is beginning to soften from the rain. And the heat. She would be warm here. I find a plastic bag and wrap the box as well as I can. However, the bag is torn and I know that it offers limited protection only.

Near the end of the largest lane leading into the square, a cacophony breaks loose. The sound is a riotous blend of firecrackers, clattering wooden noisemakers and throngs of squealing children that announces a parade of costumed little boys who appear replete in faithful renditions of archetypal vampires and blood-laden ghouls. They are solemn, yet cannot hide their joy as they march through the square.

The square half empties as people converge with the boys back down the lane. I join them, feeling strangely at peace. Our journey is not far — it leads to a small wharf where a ferry waits.

Everyone boards the ferry. It's a party. Men pass bottles of a clear, sweet-smelling liquor; children gleefully eat their candied skeletons; the women cradle their baskets and their babies. They grin as their young men send firecrackers off into the sea night.

Near the bow, an old woman sits alone. She looks at me directly, placing her hand on the bench next to her. She nods. I cross the deck and sit at her side. My mother's ashes have grown heavy.

As we near a tiny dock, the ferry's engine slows, the festive air quiets and another sound emerges from the night. For a moment I think it's a pack of dogs. Then, I recognize it as the barking of seals in their colony — the same as it sounded on the documentary I had seen months before.

It is not long before we have docked. It is no longer raining hard, but a drizzle persists.

"Isla Tiburon?" I ask.

The old woman laughs, "No, no," she says gleefully, "Isla *Eduourdo.*" Then she pauses and indicates the box. "*Que es?*" she says.

"Mother," I say, "*madre*," realizing the Spanish word for mother.

"*Venire,*" she says. She takes my hand.

We walk slowly up a hill where hundreds of others are also walking. The mood is still festive but it is mingled with a sense of sadness — of loss. Then we arrive.

At a graveyard.

Thousands of candles light the night, light the tomb-stones, and light the gathering families who assemble among the graves.

The old woman takes me near the back of the hill. We stop at a grave. She sets down her basket. She lights three candles. They illuminate the headstone. It says, "Eduourdo Fuentes", and below the name, a set of dates. He's been dead for twenty years. The old woman smiles and puts her hand over her breast. She murmurs something, nodding in the direction of the tombstone. I take it to be a prayer. She then passes three candles to me. I set down mother's ashes beside Eduourdo Fuente's grave. I light two of the candles.

While I light the third, a momumental pang of hunger suddenly reverberates within me as though I am utterly hollow. I have never felt hunger like this in my life. The old woman nods. She hands me a small loaf of bread and a small curled-up banana.

I eat with my mother. The bread soaks up my tears.

WAYS OF KILLING PEPPER

Long before Pepper, meowing in her alien tongue, and long before the big, white lights sticking out of the sky, Dad used to play the banjo. A little half smile would hang down from his nose and his face would twitch and dance along with his noisy plucking fingers. Except I think it used to wake my little sister so Mom got him to stop. Then the dog ate a hole in the skin that stretched across the banjo's metal rim and he didn't play anymore. It's that dancing face I miss most.

There are things I just can't tell my dad, especially when he knows it all and has such a hard practical bent towards reality. I can't tell my mom either, because she'll probably believe me and then I'll really be in trouble because Dad'd be peed off I didn't tell him first. So I don't tell anybody, least of all my dad because he'd laugh right in my face. He'd laugh so hard his gut'd shake. And I'd be standing there feeling like a complete idiot because I know what I saw, damn it, and it's not my fault no one would believe me. I mean, why would I make it up? You'd be stupid to make something like that up.

Dad got Pepper because he says, "the dog didn't work out," and, "cats are less trouble," but really he got her because Mom made him.

"The kids liked that dog," she said.

"I'm tired of animals underfoot all the time," he said.

"The kids need a pet," she said, and those were the final words because a couple of days later a scrawny little cat appeared in our house. It looked like it had been taken from its mother too soon. It poked around near the edge of things and meowed a lot. It was never a kitten. It went from being a scrawny little cat to being a scrawny big cat — a she cat.

Everyone remembers how Pepper got her name because she was named after Salty our dead dog. He died in the driveway after Dad drove over him coming home from work. Everyone was all sad and depressed about Dad killing Salty so that's why Mom made him get Pepper. She's the colour of pepper too and doesn't seem to mind being named after a spice. She got called worse things by Dad although he never quite tried to stuff her into a shaker.

It's a big mystery why Pepper liked Dad, especially since no one else did: she would run to him when he returned from work, rub up against him and sit on his lap at every chance she got. At first he hated her for all that but gradually he gave in and didn't seem to mind so much any more. Pepper got to the point where she would eat only the food that he had set out for her — when he remembered to set it out. It was no wonder she stayed scrawny, but it is a wonder she stayed alive. She took to trying to follow him around.

Dad drove to work one day with Pepper hiding on the nice warm engine all the way across town. He said he wondered at the howls from under the hood but thought it was just the fan belt wearing out, till he stopped, turned off the motor and the yowls kept going.

He said in his mind's eye he could see pieces of Pepper strewn about the engine, plugged into various greasy nooks and crannies — except maybe those pieces that let her make sounds like a loose fan belt.

So what did Dad do? He turned the engine back on, drove
to the nearest vet and let him open the hood of the car.

Pepper was fine. She had a singed paw.

It's a good thing Pepper has other lives to live and other
deaths to die — nine of them. She can thank Dad for
needing them all. Then she started bringing him gifts, small
things that he'd lost: coins, pens, receipts, a ring and a
diamond-studded cuff link that Dad swore he'd left at a
hotel in another town. No one saw her do it. They just
appeared at the foot of his favourite chair. She did this over
several months.

I don't understand cats.

I have a theory though — and it's not that far fetched —
that cats are extra-terrestrials, stuck here on earth; that
we're unable to communicate with them because of their
vastly superior intelligence. They try, but their purrs and
meows are incomprehensible to us. You can see it in their
eyes — they're designed for space travel. And cats can be
in two places at once — *spontaneous molecular transmigration*
— like how Scotty beams up Spock — either that or they
travel at the speed of light.

Our neighbours, the Daly's, claimed that Pepper was
dumping all over their garden. No one had ever seen the
cat do this. In fact, no one had ever actually seen the cat
enter the garden, just like no one had seen her present
those gifts to Dad. But the evidence was pretty hard to
ignore. The unmistakable stink. The stink and the feet.
Pepper was also a killer. She pulled birds out of the air and
ate them whole — except for the feet.

The inside of her mouth is ridged like a Klingon's skull.

The Daly's and Dad formed an alliance against the cat.

First Pepper was tethered.

Then she was spayed.

She didn't seem to mind being tethered. She would
lounge for hours, wrapped in one of those harness jobs they

make for cats, then she would simply disappear. We would come home and the harness would be there, but no Pepper. Eventually, she would casually reappear — bird feet littering the Daly's yard.

With her ovaries removed, Pepper cannot have kittens. Dad explained that this is to prevent the planet being over-run by cats. This, of course, is bird shit. The planet is actually being overrun by people like my dad — not by cats — although I wish birds would get a bit smarter.

Nevertheless, there's nothing as hopeless as a spayed and tethered cat who, despite all of this, still liked Dad, who still cuddled and purred, who smiled that smug cat smile when Dad was around, who finally and obnoxiously stole Dad's affection.

I was jealous. I briefly plotted her death. But that was too easy — too obvious. I came up with a better idea.

I would become a cat.

I began by eating cat food, just a kibble at a time. Then by the bowl full when no one was around. I took to licking myself and would sleep twenty hours a day. I began to stare at birds. I wondered at the texture of their tiny skulls crunching between my teeth. I pissed behind the furnace for spite. The day I shat in the garden, covering it carefully with deep black loam, Dad had me committed.

I only lasted two weeks there. The smell of hospital sheets was therapy enough for me. I'd be much more careful the next time.

It was late winter, March break to be exact, and Dad wanted to take us skiing — the whole family. He wanted to share this experience with us, his family, because he thought it would be such a good wholesome thing to do — to get away, to leave it all behind. And we could all participate — even me, in my delicate mental state.

"Anyone can ski," he said. He was an expert. He had done it twice before in his life. "You too, Lew." It would be good for me — vigorous outdoor nature mingling.

He'd asked the Daly's to look in on the house while we were away. To water the plant — we only have one — and to feed the cat. Mr. Daly smiled and said, "Of course."

Dad was the last to leave the house. He'd checked that nothing had been forgotten. He struggled to lock the front door.

The snow was swirling as we pulled out of the driveway early in the morning, but we continued. We were all dreaming of the dazzling white mountains fourteen hours away. We would shush like experts, like Dad, down the glistening slopes — except that a red light was glowing on the dashboard of the car.

Dad isn't a mechanic, even though he thinks he is. So when the car breaks down, something it does with grim regularity, he pries up the hood and stares at the engine — the oil-soaked engine. This is what experts do — except they generally know what to look for. Dad has no idea. He thinks if he stares at it long enough, the engine will start.

It never does.

It reminds me of how Salty used to stare at the back door until it opened. The only difference is that for Salty the door always opened.

Salty was smarter than Dad.

"Don't worry, we'll check it out in Grandaw," Dad said, referring to the red light on the dashboard.

Grandaw, Alberta, was the next town on the road. It's about halfway from where we live to the mountains. As we were passing through vague white hills, the car suddenly started clanging like someone beating an iron pot against a toilet bowl. Then it farted, lurched, and ground to a halt. The car was dead.

We spent three days in Grandaw waiting for the car to rise again. It was in the hands of car priests — silent men covered in grease. Mechanics. They had found a replacement engine, a transplant. The question was, would it work? No one knew. Dad traipsed back and forth across a dirty piece of prairie between the crypt-like service station and the grotty motel where we were all imprisoned together.

Just before supper on the third day, to escape Dad's making-the-worst-of-a-bad-situation and Mom's hysterical cheerfulness, I took my skis to the nearest hill. This was as good as it was going to get.

It wasn't much of a hill, in fact it was the opposite of a hill. It was a depression. A glorified ditch. I put on the skis. I skied down the ditch. I broke a ski. I fell face down in the ditch, turned over and threw a great sputtering laugh up into the darkening sky.

That was when I saw the light.

I have heard of people *seeing the light* before but I didn't know what it meant. It was so unexpected. So out of place. So stupid really. Seeing the light and it was actually that — a bright light from the sky where there was no light before.

The light swept me up and took me in. There were no voices, only a stillness that was somehow very big, like God maybe, or a UFO. Or buzzing angels. Whatever. I always thought that seeing the light was just an expression — that you understood something you didn't understand before — but that's not it at all. Seeing the light makes you realize how little you actually know. How next to absolutely nothing you know. How your body and mind are sometimes connected and sometimes not. How time and space can collapse in on themselves. And you can't explain to anyone, not even the Mounties who find you walking down the highway clutching a broken ski two hours later, blue and red lights flashing on top of their car.

"It's a miracle you're not dead," they said. It was twenty below. I was not only not dead, I showed no signs of having been outside for two hours. Red. Blue. Red. Blue. Broken light.

"Where were you?" asked Mom. She was busy packing.

"Where were you?" asked Dad. He was packing too.

"Skiing," I lied. What could I say — *seeing the light?*

"You should pack," said my sister. She was packed and waiting.

The miracle had nothing to do with me wandering the highway with a broken ski. Dad's car was running. The transplant had taken. We were going back home.

Several hours later, well past midnight, we were dragging suitcases from the car but were scarcely in the door when the neighbour, Mr. Daly appeared. He said that something tragic had happened here, tragic and inexplicable. Pepper had disappeared. Simply vanished. Her food dish had never been touched, nor her litter box and there were no tracks around the house. He was afraid she was dead somewhere: in the attic; behind the furnace; in that crawl space under the stairs. He was offering these places as though they were darknesses in his own miserable soul that needed searching to atone for his failure in looking after a cat. He felt so bad.

"The basement," said my Dad.

We all steered to the stairs. Then stopped. All of us cocking our ears at vague scratchings and meows.

In two seconds, the whole family — and Mr. Daly — were at the front door. It's actually a double door, an interior door fortified by an exterior storm door — with a six-inch space between them where Pepper had been living.

Dad struggled to pry the inner door. Something was holding it tight. He braced himself, heaved mightily and Pepper bolted into the house — along with the smell of three day's worth of semi-frozen cat shit. Five people clawed at the air, looking for a clean space to breathe.

Pepper was easy to find. The stink was strongest in my parents' room. She was hiding beneath their bed.

She was retrieved, with a broom, then taken to the bathroom.

Tasks were assigned. Mine was to clean the mess between the doors. It was remarkable how high the cat had jumped within that space. I washed dark streaks of cat shit that were shoulder high on the door. I gagged all the while.

Meanwhile, my parents bathed the cat in nice warm water. They dried her as best they could with towels. Dad attempted to complete the job with a blow dryer. Pepper took exception to this. She clamped her Klingon jaws around his thumb. Dad yelled and dropped the hair dryer. Pepper released his thumb and dropped to the floor. She walked to her food dish as calmly as she could.

Dad refused to feed her again. He made me and my sister do this. He no longer allowed Pepper to rub up against him; no longer permitted her to sit on his lap. He could not understand how he had locked Pepper between the doors. He resented the fact that a cat could make him look so stupid and be so forgiving at the same time.

"I'm not letting a *cat* run my life," he said.

Pepper grew thinner. She developed sores on her back. She licked them compulsively. They began to fester and smell. Mom took Pepper to the vet. He gave her some sort of medicinal powder. The sores got worse. Pepper weakened. She stopped eating.

She was dying.

Finally, Dad gathered the smelly, weakened cat into his arms.

"Say good-bye," he said to her. "You're an unhappy sick cat. I'm afraid your time has come."

Pepper didn't deny this. She looked at him with her dim spaceship eyes and said, "Let's go." They left.

I looked around the house at her favourite haunts, at the toys she had long since forsaken, and I missed her already. She had been so plucky and determined.

It took a day for an hour to pass.

Dad returned. He was holding Pepper.

She was still alive.

"What happened?" asked Mom.

"Where's my banjo?" asked Dad.

"Your what?"

"My banjo! My banjo! I have to play my banjo!"

"Why?" asked Mom. She was incredulous.

"We have to go to therapy," answered Dad. He had a confused look on his face. Like he'd been pinched and found out he was awake.

Pepper was purring. She was smiling.

"Animal therapy, twice a week," he said. "I'm supposed to play her music."

His face danced for a second.

Pepper laughed. She *glowed.*

Sleeping in the Nude

Graffiti is ubiquitous. It has existed forever. It has been found in Egyptian tombs, prehistoric caves and the catacombs. The word means, "scratched", but it can be painted, burnt or tattooed. So on the wall of the males' (see universal symbol for Male) school washroom, stall number three, are etched the words: *Heman sleeps in his shorts.*

"Heman" is me — a name they have given me. "Name" means "soul".

It would seem that because I have a brain and occasionally choose to use it, along with words that actually appear in the dictionary, I am often the object of extreme derision proffered at the hands of the "Torps" as I call them. Torps are people, usually male, who exist in a persistent state of *torpor*, except when setting fires to someone's bagged lunch or pulling the wings off flies — which they consider a kind of sport. In their eyes, I am a kind of fly — or possibly, a kind of bagged lunch.

The head Torp, Weez, said to me once in gym class, "Hey Heman, your shorts don't fit."

It was true, they didn't. They were way too big. I had asked for small but they gave me extra large. They looked like pajamas.

"I sleep in them," I said, trying to be convivial.

"What? You sleep in your shorts!" And he descended into paroxysms of laughter along with his friends. I did not get the joke.

So what if I sleep in my shorts? What possibly could be the problem here? Does the fact that I am a dweeb, or a dork or any term you wish to devise to describe the likes of me, determine the fact that I sleep in my shorts? And what does it mean if you sleep in the nude? That you are "cool"? Or simply cooler?

Perhaps you are like my Uncle Joe?

Uncle Joseph Mann is my father's oldest brother. He is a fireman who is about to retire. Although he is not particularly old-fashioned himself, he has an old-fashioned job and is part of my old-fashioned family, the Manns. There are an assortment of Bill, John and Mary Manns, not to mention my Uncle Joe. My own name is Harold Edward Mann, H.E. Mann — "Heman". Get it? The Torps think this is a terrific joke. Full of subtlety and wit. My parents have never acknowledged the creation of their clever acronym. I don't think they yet realize what they've done. They would certainly never recognize the significance of the name left as an identifying trademark by those who are lighting the fires.

The fires.

It was not until 1772 that a chemist by the name of Lavoisier discovered that fire was not a *thing*, but in fact a *process*. Before him, people thought that fire was a substance called *phlogiston* and that materials such as coal contained lots of it. This presumably means nothing to the fire setters in the neighbourhood. For them, fire is a recreational activity involving matches.

And yes, there have been a spate of conflagrations around the outskirts of town — old barns, outbuildings and abandoned houses — but last night, they burnt a church. At each of these fires they leave a moniker to identify themselves. The moniker is, "Heman", and no one knows what it means.

Except me. I know. I just don't know why.

Uncle Joe looks like he has been too close to too many fires for too long. He has the face of a roasted walnut. Perhaps he has also fried a bit of his frontal lobe. This would explain some of his odd habits like smoking and collecting ashtrays. And hoses. And Hogs.

By "Hogs" I don't mean pink porkers, I mean Harley Davidsons; bikes — vintage, of course — all six of which he keeps corralled in his garage. He displays, or rather, *flaunts* his vast array of crystal ashtrays as if to underscore the not-too-subtle irony of his life's vocation. The hoses he collects coil in snaky loops, ranging from diameters that children might pass through, to sizes which might admit light alone.

I don't particularly like Uncle Joe. However, he is a relative and has always managed to acknowledge me — tersely with a brittle nod and a vague flicker across his face that might be a smile. We have never had an extended conversation. There is something about him that frightens me. Maybe it's his ashtrays. Or his hoses. Or his Harleys.

He has told my father about the graffiti, "Heman", left at each of the fire sites. It's apparently burnt nearby into the ground with a propane torch. This is what Dad reported at supper. Of course I don't feel that it's appropriate to inform my parents of their stupidity regarding the acronym they built for me, and how I get called it at school. However, Uncle Joe may find the information useful.

My only decision is whether to call him at work or at home — I mean, on the one hand, it is official business, but on the other, he is my uncle.

I called him at the fire department but he was off duty. The fact that I did not give my information to whoever answered the phone, indicated something that surprised me — despite my normal feelings for him, I wanted to talk to Uncle Joe alone, to share with him this bit of stupid, self-incriminating intelligence. It was like wanting to go on a journey with someone you don't know, with no road in sight and no visible means of transportation.

After I told him the essential facts regarding Weez, the Torps and the graffiti, "Heman", the silence on the other end of the line was uncanny. I knew he was there but he was not responding.

"Hello?" I said. "Are you still there?"

He cleared his throat. "Would you like to go look?" he asked.

"Look at what?"

"At your name, the graffiti burnt in the ground."

It seemed such a strange request, I didn't know how to say no.

Uncle Joe showed up on his 1942 Harley Davidson, an antique roadster he keeps in mint shape.

"We'll go for a ride," he said.

I was hardly expecting this but it was no doubt an honour he was bestowing on me for some inexplicable reason. Or perhaps it was simply a way of avoiding conversation — talking is difficult while riding a bike. Then again, maybe he did it so he could smoke without fear of reproach.

The church, or rather, the former church and now a pile of ashes, was about fifteen minutes out of town. We drove through what is mostly farming country, interrupted by the occasional horsy acreage and/or dog kennel set flat against a red evening sky. The smell of new hay, horse barns, raw gasoline and cigarette smoke, alternating with the violence of the buffeting wind, made me feel a kind of nauseating exhilaration.

When we arrived and dismounted the bike at the charred church, my face was suddenly hot — as though the church was still fully ablaze. Uncle Joe took off his helmet and he looked more like an outlaw in his black leather jacket than someone whose job it was to save lives and preserve property. He was as unready as ever to speak. Finally, I did.

"How come you're a fireman?" I asked.

This was not an entirely shallow question; my father is a lawyer; the rest of his brothers and a sister are working professionals of some sort: two engineers, and a Queen's Court Judge.

"I like fire," was his ready response. "I'm supposed to be a *firefighter*, I mean that's the politically correct term. But really, I'm a *fire man*." He smiled one of his characteristic non-smiles.

We were walking to the front of the church and, sure enough, the graffiti was there: "Heman", scorched in three-foot high lettering, performed with ritualistic precision (I want to say "flare"). It wasn't ten metres from where misshapen globs of what had been the front door handle lay in the ashes of what had once been the door.

"Come here," said Uncle Joe, "I want to show you something."

We stepped carefully through to the middle of the church. Uncle Joe pulled aside various pieces of charred church pews and unidentifiable timbers, till finally he reached between some debris and pulled out a hymn book. He brushed it off. It was covered with soot but was unscathed by the fire.

"Something always survives. Amazing, isn't it?"

I nodded. It was amazing.

"The temperature in here would have ranged from 600 to 1,400 degrees when it was in full blaze — that's Fahrenheit. I've never been too good at Celsius."

"315 to 760," I translated almost automatically. "Roughly," I added loudly. I didn't want to show how quickly I could do math in my head.

"Warm, wouldn't you say?"

I nodded again.

"The ignition point of wood is around 400 degrees or so — hot enough to flake the skin right off you. I've seen it too, and you want to know what?"

"What?"

"We don't even know what fire is."

"Sure we do. It's when a substance combines with oxygen. It makes light and heat — fire." I was confident of that. Physics is my best subject.

"Yes, we know all that — but what *is* it? Smoke?" He was making a pun while offering me a cigarette. He actually grinned at his little joke. He had a fine smile. I had never seen it before.

I declined the cigarette. So he lit it as we strolled towards the bike. The sun poked over the horizon like a big yellow sponge — absorbing light rather than emitting it. The ride home would be a cool one.

This had been a strange, quick, flat event. We came, we looked at ashes and now we were leaving. Did he take me there to show me an unburnt book?

Uncle Joe threw his leg over the Harley saddle, hooked his boot onto the starter lever and kicked. Once. Twice. Three times — nothing. He repeated the sequence again.

"Shit," he said dismounting.

I was standing a metre or two from the bike when I noticed a small steady leak of something from the side of the engine.

"What's that?" I asked.

Uncle Joe leaned over the bike to look and a large ash dropped from his cigarette.

The explosion hit like a wave of scalding water, slamming me airborne five metres back. My eyes hurt most and I couldn't see. Nor could I hear.

But I could smell.

The scent of burning flesh.

+++

Weez and the Torps are cool. They make no connection between themselves and my lack of eyelashes and brows, as well as my singed hair. They are amused.

"Hey Heman, get too close to the barbecue?"

Indeed I did.

I go to the hospital to visit Uncle Joe. His upper body is wrapped in what looks like cellophane and gauze. He's in the shape of a human being but much of his body glistens raw. His eyes are filled with cotton batting. His mouth is a hole. He doesn't speak. He can't. I don't know if he's awake. But if he's sleeping, he's sleeping in the nude, under a plastic tent lined with white sheets. I feel ashamed and terrified to see him like this. But I also feel it's somehow my duty to be here.

Nearby on the night table is a Bible. Someone has left it there as though Uncle Joe could read through the batting on his eyes. I'm not intimate with the Bible and its terms but I am bored. It is a book. I am partial to books. Perhaps I'll read to Uncle Joe. I open it randomly, cracking the spine. I read.

The hand of the Lord God fell upon me. Then I beheld, and lo a likeness as the appearance of fire: from the appearance of his loins even downward, fire; and from his loins even upward, as the appearance of brightness, as the colour of amber. And he put forth the form of a hand, and took me by a lock of mine head; and the spirit lifted me up between the earth and the heaven, and brought me into the visions of God.

It is from Ezekiel, chapter eight, verses one to three.

"Thank you," I say. "*Fire man.*"

He stirs. I know immediately he's conscious and something has passed between us; that, whatever it is, it cannot be spoken of. I am sure that if he could smile, he would be smiling now. The reason he would be smiling is because of a perverse little joke — he now knows *what fire is*. He has collected fire with the same intensity that he has collected ashtrays and hoses and Harleys. Now his collection is complete. He has seen God.

I see only the Torps. And their burnt graffiti. I do not see God. There is no God.

There are times in your life when you are triggered into action. When you become consumed. Obsessed. Now is such a time for me.

I go to the library. I read. I read of the gods of flame: Narasamsah Agni of the Parsees, Camaxtle of the Aztecs, Svarog of the Slavs, Nusku of the Assyrians, Vahagn of the Armenians, Ulu Tojon of the Yakuts, Verethraghna of the Persians, Pele of the Hawaiians, Hephaestus of the Greeks and Vulcanus of the Romans.

I read how the Yakuts see the fire god as a gray old man; how the Hawaiians' Pele lives in a volcano; how he appears in the form of a flamed woman to warn of volcanic eruptions; how the Ostiaks refer to the god as "Fire girl" and how the ancient Egyptians believed that fire devoured its victims then died from its consummation.

I then read of fire walkers: of medieval monks, St. Polycarp, Asian shamans, Balinese trance dancers, Polynesian lava walkers, Sri Lankans of Udappawa, and the Greek Anastenarides dancing in fire on the feast of St. Constantine; how in their trance-like state they stroll barefoot across glowing coal beds unscathed, like the hymn book in the church.

I begin to understand the fire man. I believe in Uncle Joe. I formulate a plan.

◆◆◆

It is late in the school year and near grad. There will be a bush party. It is an annual event that will happen at Blueberry Flats, a place near the river. The guys will drink beer or rye. The gals will drink lemon gin or coolers. The Torps will drink beer and smoke anything they think will get them high. Someone will take their clothes off. Someone will fight. Someone will get sick.

The mosquitoes will be thickest in the shadows.

The shadows will be created by the fire.

I will create the fire.

It is near midnight. The fire pit I have prepared is about three metres by two in size and glows evenly from end to end. The fire is ready. I am ready. I slowly begin to remove my shoes and socks.

"What are you doing, Harold?" someone asks.

"I'm going for a walk," I say.

"Well then why are you taking off your shoes?"

"I'm going to walk on the fire."

A kind of rustling hush descends on the party. Even the Torps sit up. Weez grins and chuckles.

"Yeah, right. Hey Heman, if you do it, *I'll* do it," he says.

"You'd better take off your shoes," I say.

There are a few giggles — drops of water skipping across a red hot pan. There is no sense to why people laugh at times like these.

My heart is beating fast. I take a deep breath. I ease it back out. I feel my heart respond. It is mind over matter. It defies all logic. It defies physics and the rules of the real world. An act of will can do that. This is what I believe.

I step into the pit. I take three or four quick steps. It feels like hot, crunchy sand. I am through. I feel no pain. I have walked on fire.

"Your turn," I say to Weez. I toss a twig into the glowing embers. It bursts into flames.

Weez rises to his feet. He drops his beer bottle ceremoniously beside him. He grins. He steps into the fire.

He screams.

Hitler's Hands

You need know only this of me: my accompanist in Berlin was a Canadian from Montreal whose first language was neither French nor English, but a tongue that nurtured us both, Yiddish. Still, during the first two years of the war, he patiently taught me his second language, English. So if these words seem brittle and the cadence forced, forgive my wandering soul.

I will sing now, perhaps a bit muffled from where I am, but it is my way of giving — perhaps *for*giving, I am not sure. I will try not to stammer. Time has ended for me and although I bear the vague shape of my twenty years, I am much older than that. However, the body of my soul will not rest with the heartfelt plunging of a wooden stake, nor the simple brandishing of a silver cross. I am beyond all that. I will be stilled, finally, by an act of love.

Beneath Craig's bed, locked inside a khaki-coloured metal case, lie two souvenirs of the second world war: a Walther P 38, 9 mm handgun, the kind that German Officers wore, and a stick-grenade. Although there is no ammunition for the gun, the grenade is still live as far as Craig knows.

It looks like a stick with a fist-sized metal cylinder attached to the top. The top is, in fact, a small shrapnel-filled bomb. At the bottom of the stick is a metal cap. If you unscrew the cap, you see that the stick is hollow and a string with a small

weight attached to it will drop into view. This is the trigger.
If you pull the trigger, a short fuse ignites, taking four or
five seconds to burn. The idea is to throw the device before
the bomb blows your arm and head off.

The gun and the grenade were given to Craig by an uncle
who had been a soldier in WW II. He had served in a
Division of the Royal Canadian Artillery. He had been near
Oldenburg, Germany, on May 8, 1945, the day the war
ended. He said that these two things were given him by a
surrendering German Officer whom he had discovered
hiding inside the hollowed carcass of a dead horse on the
side of the road. The German Officer, he guessed, was no
more than twenty years old.

Craig's uncle did not tell Craig that he made his discovery
because he had broken from his advancing column to uri-
nate, and was mid-stream, peeing the flies off the dead
horse's eyes, when the carcass moved and a young man
emerged, half-crawling, half-sitting, cradling a khaki-coloured metal box; nor did he say, despite rumours the war
was over, that their tanks were still being pinned down by
enemy fire, and he was so frightened by the stirring horse
and the young man, that he shot him. Craig's uncle was
unable to complete urinating at the time, but he did open
the metal box.

The contents of the box caused him to gasp, for in it were
a pair of severed hands, each clutching a weapon: a pistol
and a stick grenade. He removed the body parts and returned with the two weapons exactly as they exist today.

Craig's uncle took the details of his war to the grave. He
took with him as well the restless look of resignation that
was fixed on the young German Officer's face, blood dripping down his cheeks like tears, a maggot-riddled snapshot
of the war. A snapshot that visited him nightly till he died.

Craig, though, knows none of this and the vague feeling
of discomfort he gets when he opens the box to examine

its contents passes as soon as he locks it again and pushes it back beneath his bed. Craig admires the contents of the box, the gun and the grenade, like a miser admires his hoard or a keeper his zoo. It has somehow become an extension of him, another arm or nose, no less formed but of no practical use, other than to say, "It is mine." For Craig this is important because other than his raging dreams, he possesses very little of his own.

His head is shaven, his shoulders are engraved in a serpentine frieze, his thighs show through frayed denim; his feet are shod in heavy black boots. An ancient fire-brand medallion for good fortune and freedom hangs glinting around his neck. It is known, too, as a symbol for anti-Semitism and is called a *swastika*. Only his hands betray him — silkened, long and elegant — the hands of an artist. On these he wears half-gloves — not to protect them but to hide them.

It is true that, as Craig believes, the world has treated him unfairly, that others confine his fortunes. The first of these was his father who hid his own frailty by beating Craig and his mother till there was little room between the scars. Scarred least were his hands. Craig would fit himself into a corner and draw. Others have confined him since: the school, the church, the state, till Craig perceives vast conspiracies against him. At these he wishes to lash out, to take revenge, to gain control. It is with these conspirators that he is at war. It is a holy war — a just war. A war of utter contempt. But the target has been skewed. It somehow has become the interloper: the immigrant, the minority — the Jew.

Craig finds that there are others who believe as he does, who share common deities. There is Toll, the leader; Fancy, the second, who wears a spider-web tattoo emblematic of a kill; and Credo, who believes he is God. Craig holds as much contempt for these as he does his victims.

"Heil!" says Toll, hanging his arm in a Nazi salute.

"Heil!" the others respond.

"Our mission is simple," says Toll, "to purify the species; to cleanse. The process doesn't matter. It must be done; exterminate . . . "

"Hey!" says Fancy.

"Subjugate and purge," Toll continues. "To purify the race is the ultimate goal."

It is not unreasonable this process of purification. It is nature's way. It assures survival. It accounts for history. It accounts for the determination of nation states; for maps; for greed. It does not account for acts of love. It does not account for art.

Of art too little is said. For although it binds its maker into doubt and uncertainty, it completes a sense of time. It evokes the dead. It gives hope. It is an act of love.

That is why Craig wears gloves. Craig has a rare talent. When he draws one line, it is a quick irreverent stroke. When he joins that line with another, and another, it becomes, instantly, a thing of beauty; the flaring nostril in the head of a horse; the sinewed neck leaning into the wind. He has no awareness of this talent, no conscious control. It is just something he can do. It places him in history, for, he believes, Hitler had the same talent.

Craig, of course, is wrong. The passion and vigour that Craig exploits to render kicks and blows, he reinvents again into contoured shades of light and dark. Adolf Hitler, in fact, did not have the same talent, although he aspired to it. He did draw in his early days, painting vague lifeless water-colours for frame merchants who found their wares sold better if there was something — anything — between the borders. But Hitler's hands were not for painting. They had other designs.

Cola di Rienzi was a fourteenth century Italian patriot. He also managed to become a dictator, which is not so unusual in itself because every leader in those days was a dictator of some sort. However, two things make Cola unique: he achieved his goal of being dictator, not once but twice; the second time, he was slain, stoned to death by those he would rule. Wilhelm Richard Wagner, the 19th century composer, most famous for a passage from *Die Walküre*, wrote an earlier opera, *Rienzi*, that glorified Cola as a hero — a peasant who rises to become a great leader. The addendum to this is that the *Rienzi* opera was Adolf Hitler's favourite.

Craig knows nothing of Cola di Rienzi or Hitler's tastes for opera, but as Hitler admired the romanticized story of the fourteenth-century dictator, Craig admires Hitler. It seems to Craig that Hitler always wore gloves in his public appearances. Craig assumes that Hitler too wished to hide his hands. This may have been true, to a point. Hitler wore gloves to avoid uncertain contamination from the people that he ruled.

Craig lies on his bed. His eyes are closed and though he is exhausted, he is not asleep. His heart still races. He is slightly drunk. Beneath his half-gloves, his knuckles are swollen. There is blood on his boots. He has helped beat a man to within an inch of his life — if life can be measured that way.

The man Craig has beaten is a musician. His name is Aaron Lauterman and would be my nephew if I were alive. I feel the pain of my nephew Aaron, who, in fact, bears my name. I am angered and vengeful, but powerless. What, after all, can a spirit do?

Aaron has virtually no knowledge of me or the name we share. It means, "slow to speak", and true to our names, we both are. Stutterers. Aaron's mother (who would be my sister, Zosia) remembers me as a sound or perhaps, more correctly, as a series of sounds. My sister holds this memory because I too am a musician, a singer, and it is my voice she hears. When I sing, I never stutter.

I am humming now for her. The melody is a Romanian folk song our mother used to sing. It has since been refashioned into an anthem for the state of Israel. She is barely conscious of it as happening. It is music playing in her head. She tries to think of me, to form a face, but she cannot.

Craig, on the other hand, is startled. His eyes open wide. He can hear my voice as though it is in his room. And, in truth, it is — albeit confined to the space of a metal box containing a gun and stick grenade.

I stop humming. Craig listens, unsure. His eyes dart around the room. He is sitting up now. He wonders if he is "hearing things". He decides it must be a radio or TV from another part of the building. He lies back down. I begin again, this time singing the arias of *Rienzi*. The melody rises like a bloated corpse. The words shift like lead, heavy and awkward. Craig knows *the sound is real* and that it comes from within his room.

He is on his knees; his boot-toes scuff across the dirty thin linoleum. His medallion digs bluntly into his sternum and his elbows poke cold and gristly as he leans into the floor, reaching beneath the bed to pull out the box.

When he opens the case, I stop singing. I feel my vague shape becoming less so. I begin to fill space with something resembling light. To Craig, it appears that someone has beamed a flashlight into his eyes. He lurches back from the light and cracks his bald skull against the bed frame.

I laugh.

It is the first time I have laughed in more than fifty years. It feels astonishingly good, as though I have witnessed the skilled performance of a clever, cruel joke. I laugh some more.

But Craig does not understand and is scowling in pain. There is a deep red gash where his head struck the frame and blood runs freely down his back, though he is not yet aware of this.

I am sitting on the edge of Craig's bed, behind him. He is holding the back of his head, trying not to pass out.

"You're b-b-b-b . . . You're bleeding," I say. I am rather surprised that even in my present form I still stutter.

Craig turns so sharply that a brilliant half-circle of blood is spun off in a string of red beads. Then a small involuntary yelp releases from his throat as he scuttles frantically to make distance between us.

"Who the hell are *you?*" He asks this as though I have asked the same question first.

The ghost or spirit of whatever I am is typically reticent now, speaking in epigrams or lofty puzzles. But I am not like that. I have come for simple retribution.

"My name is Aaron Lauterman," I sing. "You b-b-b-beat my ne-ne-ne . . . My nephew," I say.

Craig now blinks hard. He is wondering if what he sees in front of him is real. He is wondering how a stuttering young man wearing the uniform of a German officer from the second world war can be in his room; how this young officer can be Aaron Lauterman's uncle.

"Get out of here," Craig snarls.

"I c . . . ," I start to say.

"Yes, you can," he anticipates for me.

" . . . Ant," I say.

He flings a chair at me. It crashes against the wall. I am visible, but not physical. He kicks, swings and punches. But of course, nothing happens — to me. Craig, on the other hand, is growing exhausted. He is still losing blood.

"You should take c . . . are of that," I say, referring to his head.

"Get out!" Craig screams. "Get out, get out, get out!"

He flips the bed onto its side while I remotely ascend aloft. He watches, taking two steps backwards, then collapses onto the floor. As unconscious as clay.

When Craig awakes, lying on the floor amid random splatters of coagulated blood, he is unsure of his memory. He recalls vaguely the vision of a stammering youth in army garb. He wonders about hearing voices. He has a sharp pain on the back of his head. He is hungry.

It is exquisite, this pain: this hunger. It sharpens him, enables him to focus clearly on the enemy. Look what they have done to him, his enemies. They have filled him with pain. They have defiled his home with blood — his blood.

Craig meets with his allies — with Toll, Fancy and Credo. They marvel in their way at the open battle wound on the back of Craig's head. It is a swollen red gash, an angry banner. Craig does not tell them about his apparition nor the true manner in which he received the lesion — that he banged his head on a bed frame. It is all the same. It is a wound caused by an enemy. They plot new revenge.

They will bomb the home of Aaron Lauterman.

To build a bomb is not difficult, less difficult than to build peace. But it is simpler yet when one exists waiting for use. Craig has such a bomb in a metal box beneath his bed. They will not use it today, nor tomorrow. They will wait instead till Aaron the musician is released from hospital. There is no point in bombing an empty house. They know where he lives. They have found his address in the telephone book and three of them take turns keeping the house under surveillance.

Toll owns an ancient VW van. Its curdled cream colour accentuates the rust flaking away from the wheel wells and beneath the van's doors. It is from the van that they keep their watch in four-hour shifts.

Craig is half-way through his first watch. It is ten P.M. He is listening to the radio and drinking a coke. It is quiet, a quiet street with older houses sitting on treed lots. I approach from the other end of the block; Craig stirs. I pass beneath a street light. I am wearing the uniform. I know this will quicken Craig's heart. He stiffens himself into the van's seat, trying to conceal himself from me. I draw closer and closer.

Craig recognizes me — the youth who visited him in his room, the one who said he was Aaron Lauterman's uncle. As I pass, I freeze Craig by looking him in the eye. I present the small gift of a smile, then I am gone.

Craig scrambles out of the van to assail me, but I am no longer in his sight.

He is perplexed, shaken. He is no longer sure if it was a smile or a grimace that I wore. But he can see it clearly in his mind. He wants to draw my face, to fix it on paper, to lock it into time and space. To study it. The impulse is so overpowering that he cannot resist. He must do it, now. Tomorrow may be too late — though too late for what, Craig is not sure. He is only sure that he cannot delay. Except that he has no paper, no surface upon which to lay ink or lead or charcoal or paint. Or the markings from a felt pen.

There is a box of them in the van, felt pens for distinguishing the sides of things, usually buildings, with slogans, graffiti and other declarations of war.

Craig moves the van closer to the street light. He takes the pens and exits the van. The side of the van, above the rust, becomes a canvas. He draws, under the street light, part of the face: the nose, the mouth, the chin. It is the smile he is after, or is it a grimace? He draws the mouth again and again. He covers the van with mouths. His drawings stutter. He cannot get it right. The shapes elude him. My face is gone.

When he sees the VW van, Toll is confused, angry.

"What's this?" he wants to know. "You got *mouths* all over my van."

"I was trying to get it right," says Craig, pretending that it's a joke.

"*Mouths!*" repeats the owner. "Are you trying to say something, Craig? Like, is this *art?*"

"I don't know," says Craig.

"You wrecked my van, a-hole."

"I'll paint it," says Craig.

He cannot explain. He cannot explain how the lines would not go together, how there was something missing in the light.

During his next watch, twelve hours later, Craig has brought paper and he has brought pens. He tries to sketch my full body as I sit in his memory — as I sat on his bed. But it too is wrong. There is no substance or shape. He cannot get it right.

Suddenly, Craig sees me, the young soldier again. I sit on the front step of my nephew's house. On my lap is a metal box, a khaki-coloured metal box like the one under Craig's bed. I stare out towards the street then slowly rise, turn and look at Craig. As I look, I begin my way up the steps towards the door of the house. I hold the metal box close to my chest.

Craig grabs the stick grenade, bolts from the van and races across the street. He runs towards me, watches me as I reach for the front door, open it and enter the house.

Craig dashes up the steps, grabs the door handle and pulls. He expects the door to open. It does not. He shakes the door. The window panes rattle. "Talk to me!" he screams at the locked door. "Talk to me!"

I cannot talk to Craig. What would I say to him? How would I say it, besides slowly? And what effect would it have? What would he believe? What would he care that a Jewish boy with a stutter should end up replacing the bowels of a dead horse, carrying a metal box, wearing the uniform of a German officer on the last day of the Second World War?

"Talk to me!" he screams again and smashes through a pane of glass with the stick grenade. He reaches through the broken glass and turns the doorknob.

He finds no one, certainly not Aaron, though I am humming one of the sad arias of *Tosca*. It is as close as I can come to him for the moment. However, placed precisely in the centre of the floor of the living room is a khaki-coloured metal box. He recognizes the box. It is the same as the one under his bed.

I stop singing as he opens the box. In it, lying bloodless and cold, are a pair of severed hands. Their tapered fingers are long, exquisite and sheathed in white gloves.

Craig takes two steps back. He looks about the room. I appear. He looks at me and smiles. I do not return the gift, but I do nod, acknowledging.

Craig unscrews the cap on the stick grenade.

He is creating the perfect vision of how light determines the shape of things.

THE CODE

You could almost taste the blood as coach Lamb slammed a stick against the wall. "Skate!" he screamed, "Cut their legs off!" He threw the stick onto the floor. "You do that, and you'll win."

And we did. And we won.

We took our winning everywhere. We were used to getting our way. So to celebrate our first place finish, we went to *Dezzie's*, a nightclub. Some of us were already inside when there was a commotion at the door. We investigated. The bouncer had asked one of the team for ID.

The sound of a beer bottle breaking against someone's skull is not like you hear it in the movies. Nor is the sound of his head hitting the ice-coated pavement. And you never see the shards of glass mingled with blood, beer and hair on frozen snow. You know he is still alive because he is blowing small red bubbles through his nose.

And when the police come, you say nothing. You saw nothing. Not because you are afraid of ending up like the bouncer on the sidewalk, but because there is a code: *no one tells on a teammate.* And you are on the team.

I am on the team. My grandfather watches. "Good game," he says, "just have fun." He says it if we win or lose. He stands at the corner of the rink. He is always there. It does not matter how cold it is. It does not matter that he is not alive. He is always there.

Coach Lamb has called a meeting. We are supposed to have a practice tonight but it has been cancelled. It's just him and us — he doesn't even let D'Arcy in the room and D'Arcy's the trainer who never misses a thing.

"All right guys." He steps between the hockey bags strewn about the dressing room. His head is down — thinking of the right words to say — his finger is to his lips. "Close the door, Mike."

I close the door.

"Now we've been through a lot this year. We've won the division, and now we're going to playoffs. I'm proud of you. It's not every year I get to do this. It takes a special kind of chemistry. And this team — you — have got that chemistry. There's no reason why we can't go all the way."

A couple of the animals give a half-hearted "Yeah!"

Coach Lamb looks at them. They look down between their feet. He continues.

"But what happened the other night, never should have happened. I don't care if you went out and had a few drinks to celebrate and I don't even care if you give some guy a knuckle sandwich — that's going to happen from time to time — but I draw the line at trying to put a beer bottle into someone's head! That is where I draw the line. That is criminal activity. And I don't support criminal activity — this team does not support criminal activity.

"Now I don't care which one of you did that, I don't even want to know — that's not why I called this meeting — because as far as I'm concerned, you're all guilty! Every one of you is guilty — even those of you who weren't there, *because you should have been there.* Whether you were there or not, you get tarred with the same brush. So don't any of you go thinking you're better than anybody else, because you're not. None of you.

"What I'm going to do right now is I'm going to leave this room with you in it. And you're going to decide among yourselves what you're going to do about this thing. It's all up to you. Whatever decision you come up with — that's it. You got to live with it. For the rest of your lives."

Coach Lamb nods, "For the rest of your lives." With that, his eyes stop at two or three people in the room. One of them is me. It's just for a split second, but there's a look in his eyes that does not fit. It's not right. He grunts as he pushes open the door and leaves.

We all sit there, staring up or down or at blank spaces on the wall. No one looks at the guy who did it, even though we all know.

Jay, our captain, feels like he's got to break the ice. "So now what?" he says.

The words rattle around the room. No one says anything. But one of the rookies, Chris, fidgets like something inside him is trying to get out. Finally, he speaks.

"I think the guy who done it should own up." Chris is one of the guys who was not there that night.

"We're all in it together," says Jay. "You heard the coach."

"They're going to find out anyway — sooner or later," says Chris.

"Yeah? Who's going to tell, you?" taunts Jay.

Chris does not answer. He just fidgets some more.

"I didn't think so," says Jay.

What follows is a long silence. We are all thinking *there is no way out of this*. We are all wishing "the guy who done it" would indeed own up. But he isn't saying anything. He is a team player.

Up to now, it's been fun. The whole season has been fun. It's been fun because we've been winning. There is nothing like it. To be on a winning team. And we are used to winning, we have become accustomed to being better than everyone else. Even when we occasionally lose, we know we are better — superior. That is because *we make losers*.

Kyle whispers something to Chris. Chris shrugs his shoulders. You can almost see a little bubble of an idea rise above their heads.

"What are you guys talking about?" asks Jay.

"Nothing," says Kyle.

"Nothing?" Jay is not ready to let this little bubble go unburst.

"Kyle thinks we should get a lawyer."

Everyone looks up, first at Chris and Kyle, then at Jay.

Jay nods, "Yeah," he says real slow, "good idea."

The whole room comes to life, like this is the answer to everything — water to the thirsty. A lawyer. A *team* of lawyers. That will take care of the situation. Let justice take its course. Justice says that winners will win. And, of course, we are all winners.

Jay calls the coach back into the room and as he enters it suddenly occurs to me what I saw in his eyes, because I see it again. It is pure joy. Happiness. We are truly a team. We will do anything to win.

"Lawyers, eh?" says coach Lamb. "Okay, lawyers it is," he smiles, "but I got a question for you." He looks around the room. "Who's going to pay for them? Who's going to pay for the snakes to get you off the hook? I tell you one person who is not going to pay for them. *I'm* not going to pay for them. It's your decision. *You* are going to pay for them. Your parents are going to pay for them, or whoever else you can con. But not me. I'm just doing my job with you guys. So then, that's your decision."

"That's our decision," says Jay.

"Good . . . I only got one more thing to say. A good team overcomes adversity. A good team meets all the challenges, a good team finds a way to win. That's what we've done all year, and that's what we're going to continue to do — that's what we have to do — because if we don't, they are going to cut our legs off. Okay? You got that? So, let's put this behind us then. Only a good team can become a championship team."

The room cheers. Or, rather, the people in it do — the room is actually very quiet. The room knows.

"I did it," I mumble.

"What?" Coach Lamb is stunned.

"I did it," I say louder.

"You did *what?*" demands the coach.

"I hit the guy with the beer bottle," I say.

The coach looks at me. "Did you," he smiles, "alone?"

I nod. "On the head," I add.

Coach Lamb looks around the room. "Mike says he hit the guy with a beer bottle. On the head. I want to ask the rest of you guys if Mike did this alone. I want you to think very carefully if Mike did this alone, because if Mike is part of the team — Mike couldn't have done it alone."

Again, coach Lamb looks around the room. Like he is searching. "I personally find it very difficult to believe that Mike did this *alone.*"

An air vent, which has been blasting hot air into the room all this time, shuts off. It is suddenly very quiet. You can hear Coach Lamb breathing.

Chris looks up. The Rookie. He stares the coach in the eye.

"I did it," says Chris.

The coach raises his eyebrows.

"*I* did it," says Jay, the captain.

The coach looks at him.

"It was me," says Kyle.

The coach opens his mouth.

"No, I did it," says the next guy. And so on, all around the room.

Then they all cheer. Again.

Coach Lamb smiles openly.

✦✦✦

We lose the first game in the playoffs.

Grandpa is still standing at the corner of the rink.

"It's not a game anymore," says coach Lamb, "it's a fight. It's a fight to prove that you're the best. That you can overcome any obstacle to prove that you're the best. Don't worry about anything off the ice. That'll take care of itself."

He is referring to the fact that a court date has been set for a preliminary hearing. It has been set for after the playoffs. The lawyer and the judge are team players.

Grandpa had been a judge.

Even though Grandpa was lying in his hospital bed, hooked up to machines that kept track of his feeble heartbeats, he still watched hockey. When he wasn't watching it, he was reading about it. When he wasn't reading about it, he was talking about it. He couldn't get enough. It was a year ago during the Stanley Cup playoffs and some of the dark horses — teams that no one expected anything from — were doing pretty well. I said as much.

"*Teams* don't make it to the NHL," he said, "*individuals* do. The only problem is, you got to be part of a team and that's a tricky thing because *it can beat you up.*"

I didn't hit the guy because he did anything to me personally or because I was defending myself or even because he insulted me. I hit him because he was insulting the team. That's why I hit him.

Nobody quits a hockey team. You get hurt or traded, or maybe waived. But not now, not at this time of year when you are in the playoffs. It's unheard of. And if you did want to quit, you would never say, "I want to quit." No, you would not say that. You would use the code. Every team has a code. On our team the code is this: *I want the key to the stick room.*

I screw up my courage. I go to the coach's office. I knock on the door.

"Come in," says the coach.

"I want the key to the stick room," I say.

Coach Lamb looks up from some paperwork he is doing. He slides his glasses down his nose. "Mike," he says, "don't bother me now. And close the door when you leave."

I am not ready for this abrupt dismissal. I am stunned. I turn and leave. I close the door.

The thought occurs, *I will go to D'Arcy.*

I find him in the laundry room. He is sorting sweaters. However, before I can open my mouth, he ambushes me, accusing me of theft.

"Where's the stick saw?" he says as soon as he sees me. He is very attached to the stick saw, largely because it seems to go missing when he wants it most. He carries it with him, along with the med bag, almost everywhere he goes.

"I don't know," I say.

"Well you had it last."

"No I didn't."

"Yes you did. I saw you doing three sticks in a row."

"That wasn't me, that was Kyle."

"Well where the hell is *he?*"

"How should I know?"

"I'm sick of buying stick saws for you guys. You want a stick saw, buy your own!"

"I didn't take your stick saw!"

"What the hell do you want then?"

"The coach says to give me the key to the stick room."

"Bullshit," says D'Arcy. "If he wanted you to quit, he'd tell me."

People always tell you that quitting is easy. That you can just walk away. But you can't. There are routes you have to take. Quitting is as hard as starting, maybe harder. It is a *process*, not an event. Quitting is a way of changing who you are.

So how am I going to do it?

If I can't quit, then I'll have to do something so bad, so reprehensible that I'll get kicked off the team. The question is what. Clearly, if assault is not enough, then what *is*? Manslaughter? Murder?

I'm not a murderer, that's the problem. I'm a hockey player who can't quit a hockey team. I don't know how. I should wear pink. Pink laces. With pink tape on my stick. I will. I will get laughed off the team.

I wear pink. In the dressing room, the guys laugh.

I wear pink. On the ice. I score three goals, including the winner in OT.

Next game, we go on the road. *Everyone* wears pink laces. Pink tape. We lead the series two games to one.

I am a hero.

The coach smiles.

Quitting is hard.

Grandpa is still standing at the corner of the rink.

◆◆◆

One more win and we are in the finals. We will win the fourth game at home.

It is near midnight and we are on the team bus, waiting to continue our trip home. We have stopped at a roadside gas station somewhere in the middle of nowhere. The team has settled from its adrenaline rush, although occasional clusters of laughter erupt from the rear of the bus. D'Arcy climbs aboard, clutching the med bag and his stick saw in its special little sling. He sits across from coach Lamb dozing in his seat a third of the way back. I like sitting right at the front, beside the door, and I sit there now.

The bus is running and we are waiting for the driver. He has gone to the can or something and must be constipated because there is no sign of him.

Somebody yells from the back of the bus, "Hey Mikey! You drive!" He is joking, of course. But I suddenly realize this is a gift. My chance to do something *so bad.*

I look back and give a half-salute, then casually settle into the driver's seat. Those who can see me, laugh. They keep on laughing as I close the door. Then I put the bus in gear and we begin to move. Shrieks and hollers join the laughter. A chant emerges.

"Go, Mike, go! Go, Mike, go!"

The driver is running alongside the bus. He goes to bang on the door but slips. Falls. I watch him through the rearview mirror. He gets to his feet, swiping at the snow on his knee, growing smaller. He quickly disappears into the darkness as I pick up speed.

D'Arcy shakes the coach.

The coach suddenly realizes what actually is going on.

"What the hell is he doing?" He scrambles to his feet.

I didn't realize how easy these buses are to drive. I'm doing eighty klicks in no time.

"Mike, what the hell are you doing! Stop!" Coach Lamb is standing beside me now.

I am wondering how fast this thing will go. The speedometer only goes to 140. I'm just approaching 100.

"Stop!" screams the coach. He grabs the steering wheel.

Now this is a mistake. Only one person at a time can drive. He tries to jam his foot on the brake. He in fact presses mine onto the accelerator. A car is coming. We are on the wrong side of the road. I yank the wheel to avoid the oncoming car. We swerve.

We are airborne.

In that moment before we land, there is only the roar of the diesel engine spinning tires at nothing but air. It is also in that moment that I have the absurd realization that I am no longer on the team. That there might not be much team left.

Then, a violent, shuddering, chaotic tumble filled with the grinding heave of metal and glass, till, like the carcass of some great dead thing, it lurches onto its side. Followed by one breath of terrified stillness.

"Shit," somebody says.

"Anybody hurt?!" Jay hollers. "Is everybody okay?"

I count my limbs. I feel my head. I know I can see, but only through one eye. Other than that . . .

"My leg," someone moans.

"Jim's bleeding," says someone else.

"Turn off the engine!" screams Jay.

The motor is still running. Diesel fumes fill the air. I find the key. Turn it off.

In the next five minutes, everyone is accounted for. Alive and climbing or being pushed through the emergency exit of what is now the top of the bus.

Everybody that is, but the coach. His leg is caught in some tangle of metal near the front door and although I have placed my jacket over him, he is shaking violently. D'Arcy is trying to free him. He can't. I am crouched behind D'Arcy trying to help, but really, I am doing nothing.

Besides shaking, Coach Lamb is wailing a single, high, thin note that increases and decreases in intensity with each breath he takes. Between these wails are guttural curses directed at us — at me really. It is a mixture of anger and pain. I have never heard sounds like these before.

An acrid smoke is beginning to fill the bus.

Jay is trying to smash the front windshield of the bus to make it easier to remove the coach. The windshield is, miraculously, still intact.

"Fire! There's a fire starting!" yells Jay. "Hurry up!"

The coach suddenly becomes quiet. And still. "Cut my leg off," he says to D'Arcy.

"What?" D'Arcy can't believe what he has heard.

"My leg, cut it off."

D'Arcy swallows, "How?" he says.

"Your stick saw," says the coach.

"I can't," says D'Arcy.

"Do it," says coach Lamb.

"I couldn't," says D'Arcy.

"I'm going to die if you don't," says the coach.

D'Arcy freezes. Stiff. Small flames begin to appear at the back of the bus.

"Give it to me," I hear myself say.

D'Arcy looks at me. He reaches for the med bag and detaches the saw from its sling. He hands it to me. He then ties a tourniquet around below coach Lamb's knee. We trade places. I grip the saw and look at the coach.

"Are you ready?" I ask.

"Nobody wants to lose a foot, Mike," he says.

"I know."

Then he looks at me like he sees me for the first time. "You really did hit that guy with the bottle, didn't you," he says.

"Yes," I say.

"You're going to make it, Mikey," he says.

"I know," I say.

My grandfather stands at the back of the bus.

D'Arcy gets sick when I hit into the bone.

THE APPRENTICE

Most people have a pair of grandmas tidily divided between their mom and dad. I had two from my dad alone: Grandma Vera and Grandma Nadia. Grandma Nadia was not technically my grandmother in a blood sense but she lived with Grandma Vera like my mom used to live with my dad. If you get the picture.

I'm assuming this. I don't know it for a fact. What can you know about two old ladies, one of whom died drunk? The other, though, is quite alive. She has pink hair, chain-smokes and believes in Elvis. Her hair got that way when she tried to dye it red. I take her shopping and for rides now that I have my licence. She appreciates it, especially since they took away hers. Grandma Vera.

Grandma Vera knows that Elvis is alive because she saw him at Super Valu. "He shows up at the Mall a lot," she says. No one believes her. It's hard to believe an old lady with pink hair. She doesn't care. I believe her. I don't want to — I have to.

"Visions are no big deal," she says. "You have to know how to look."

"What do I want to have visions for?"

"So you can see."

"See what?"

"The future."

"I don't want to see the future."

"If you don't want to see the future, maybe you'll see the past — how should I know?"

Arguing is pointless. Her sense of logic defies analysis. It just *is*. She is a sorceress of sorts and, by her appointment, I am her apprentice.

Grandma Vera is not politically correct. She calls Brazil nuts, niggertoes, and First Nations People, Indians or half-breeds, not bothering to distinguish. She calls Jewish people Jews, and uses the same word to describe someone who has cheated or stolen, as in, "He jewed me out of a ten." She calls old women, girls, and old men, farts. She means well. She no longer calls Chinese people chinks, although she still refers to Mandarin oranges as Japs.

She called Grandma Nadia, "The DP".

"When the DP showed up, I didn't know anything," she says. "All I knew was I was alone. We were both hooked on the same man, and he buggered off." She laughs her smokey laugh. "Pretty funny, eh? But she showed me a lot. She showed me everything. How to see — everything. I miss that drunken old DP."

Just as quickly as she laughed, her eyes turn rheumy and hover on the edge of tears.

Grandma Nadia had come from "the old country", and she was supposed to marry my grandfather who'd disap-peared. If I ever see him, I'm supposed to "kick him where it hurts." These are Grandma Vera's instructions.

I never got any instructions from Grandma Nadia. She never spoke much and what little she said was thickly coated in a vodka accent which made her all but indecipherable. She really did die drunk. I was about twelve. Grandma Vera said her liver gave out. Cirrhosis. She left a space in the universe where she might have been if she didn't drink so much. But that's what happens to the dead — they leave room for the rest of us.

The funeral was short and sweet. There were no eulogies. None. Grandma Vera wouldn't allow them. I was glad, but a great gloom settled into my dad, so severe that he wound up in the hospital — on the fifth floor where the windows are barred. When he got out, he left my mom and me, as though we were somehow to blame. Maybe we were.

My life was split then, as neatly as a tennis court — one week with Mom then one week with Dad. Shared custody. When I was sixteen, I got to choose between them for a full-time home. I chose Mom.

I would have chosen Grandma Vera, but it wasn't an option.

✦✦✦

Grandma lives alone now and gets bored tucked in her little clapboard house. I visit her there. She tells me to take her for a ride. Being dutiful (and bored myself) I take her this evening out onto the prairie on some back roads near the river. She is going on about a dog she had that used to kill the neighbour's chickens. I don't know why she is telling me about this. She has never mentioned it before.

But she likes to talk and I like to listen.

"Ray just about didn't make it to his third birthday," she says. "He got hit by a car and was in a coma for three weeks. With any luck at all, he would have died." She cackles. Ray is my dad.

"Grandma, that's not nice," I say.

"*He's* not nice," she says.

"I'm glad you've accepted who you are," Grandma told him after he got some kind of an award for walking twenty-five thousand miles (in twenty years). "I'm just sad you've rejected who you might have been." He could play anything with strings. She wanted him to be a musician. "He was very good. He went to Nashville but never stuck it out." He delivers mail instead.

I have pulled over to the side of the road and we are eating chicken sandwiches that Grandma has made. She thinks I still like Kool-Aid because I liked it when I was six. She is pouring some from a thermos into a paper cup. It is grape. It will leave a purple stain around my mouth. My mom will know I have been visiting Grandma.

We see a distant figure on the road. In the half light of the setting sun, we cannot discern whether the shape is man or beast. We sip our Kool-Aid. We decide that it is a beast. A horse.

It is not so unusual to see a horse around here. This is the west. People have horses. But this horse is alone. Usually they travel in groups, *herds*. It is approaching us directly. If it doesn't stop, it's going to march right over top of my car.

The horse stops — its nose hanging over the hood. It's not a big horse and a magnificent sheen from the setting sun plays off its dusty roan coat.

"What does it want?" I whisper.

"I don't know," but it sounds like, "Uh-oh-ooh," because she is chewing vigorously on her chicken sandwich. She still has several of her own teeth.

"Does it want us to move?"

"Uh-oh-ooh," says Grandma.

"Why doesn't it just go around?"

It really does look as though the horse is waiting for us to move. I get out of the car.

"Ho boy," I say, cheerily.

The horse nods.

I have never attempted a conversation with a horse before. I don't know the language — except for "giddup" and "whoa", neither of which is appropriate here. There's "gee" and "haw" for left and right, but I forget which is which.

The horse stands there. It says nothing. I am uncomfortable with the silence of strangers. When the strangers are horses, I am confused as well.

"Nice day — er, evening," I say. "Are you going to move, or what?"

Another pause. Like neither of us can figure out what to do next. Or, like we're enjoying the evening air together — which we are. Except for the bugs. With a swoosh of its tale, the horse dismisses a horde of gathering mosquitoes.

It whinnies.

"Do you want a sandwich?" I offer.

The horse looks at me like it's thinking about it.

"Just kidding," I say.

Then off in a field of wheat lying next to the road, the dim figure of a young woman suddenly calls, "Duchess! Duchess!"

The horse immediately turns, tosses its head and gently murmurs. It shuffles down into the ditch, springs lightly over a barbed-wire fence towards the figure in the field. They soon both fade into the sea of wheat and gathering night.

I have the most extraordinary feeling that the woman in the field was Grandma Nadia.

I climb back into the car. Grandma Vera is lighting up a smoke.

"I wonder what that was all about?" I say.

"That was a vision," she says.

"A what?"

"A vision," she says, blowing a blue cloud. "I'm teaching you how to see them."

"But it was so real."

"Of course it was real. What do you expect?"

That was the first one.

✦✦✦

Grandma Vera went into the hospital for two days last week. She had tests. I doubt if she's going to flunk. She can still sprint ten yards with a shopping cart trying to sneak into a checkout line. Into the back of some poor slob's heels. When I grow old, I hope I'm just like her — well, a male version. She's going to be seventy-five next month.

She calls my dad "the mailman". They can't stand each other. When one speaks, the other responds in grunts or single syllables, like they have said all there is to say between them. I don't know what history determines this relationship. I don't particularly care but I am curious.

It is hard to imagine Dad as a musician. (He is a "letter-carrier", to be politically correct.) He trudges around town assaulting mailboxes with junk mail and bills. In summer, he wears shorts so he can tan his knees. In winter, he looks like a snowbound version of the grim reaper, all hoods and folds.

His idea of a good time is collecting rocks. Like Bert, on *Sesame Street.* He has enough stone in the basement to ballast the *Queen Mary.* If there's ever an earthquake, his house will be too heavy to shake, although it might sink straight to hell.

My mother is an RN, a nurse. She has a hobby akin to Dad's. She *makes* rocks. She takes mud and turns it into stone. Pottery. This would be as close as they get to communicating.

It strikes me that no one communicates with Dad — at least no one I know. Certainly not me. The one thing my mom and I used to do is talk. We did this in the garage where her workshop is. She would turn pots and I would sit nearby on an old over-stuffed easy chair and we would talk. I can't remember what we talked about but it was very relaxing. We don't do it any more. I don't know why.

"I miss talking to you, Mom."

She looks up from her pot, "I miss listening," she says.

"Did you know Dad when he was a musician?"

"No, I didn't. I didn't know he played anything till a long time after we met."

"How come he quit?"

"There was no point, he said, after Elvis died."

"After Elvis died."

"Yes, he said he jammed with him."

"He jammed with Elvis? When?"

"I don't know. Some time or other, he said."

"Wow. That's incredible."

"Yes it is, isn't it. And that's why I don't believe a word of it."

"You don't?"

"Your father is crazy, Kyle — you know that. He was crazy long before Nadia died." She is referring to his stint in the hospital.

I do know he's a bit loopy. It just never quite dawned on me before. It occurs to me that perhaps it runs in the family — like big teeth or red hair.

"Shit," she says. The pot she's been working on suddenly goes all wobbly, collapsing.

"I'm seeing things, Mom," I say to her.

"What?"

"I see things — have visions."

"What do you mean?" she asks.

"From Grandma," I say. "She's teaching me. But I don't know if it's real."

"What kind of visions?" she asks.

"I saw a horse, and a woman. I think it was Grandma Nadia."

"Do you want to see a doctor?" she asks.

"No, Mom, I don't want to see a doctor." I get up from the chair and leave. Now I know why we don't do this any more.

The day has become so crystal clear and bright that colours are edged like knives. You are afraid that if you touch them, they will cut you. And you'll stand around bleeding, wondering why the colours are so sharp. So to dull the stupid colours, you do a trick with your eyes to fool them. You squint.

I have picked up Grandma to take her shopping, but she didn't want to go. She wanted to visit a friend in hospital. On the way there, I tell her about the conversation with Mom. About Dad jamming with Elvis.

"Elvis who?"

"Presley, the guy you keep seeing at the mall."

"I've never seen him at the mall."

Maybe her mind is starting to go. Or maybe it's mine. I drop her off at the front door of the hospital. She says she will take a cab home and not to worry about her. She plods up the steps carrying a paper shopping bag. She looks old and frail.

I am squinting, waiting on 8th Street for a sharp red light to change. There is one car in front of me. There is no one on either side. My car belonged to my mom. She gave it to me for my seventeenth birthday. For this, I am endlessly and lovingly grateful. What a shitty reason to love your mom. Dad does not drive.

A car pulls up beside me, easing its way to the crosswalk. It is an old black Lincoln Continental. The driver has long, slicked-back, black hair.

The light changes. The car in front of me surges ahead. The Lincoln is slow off the mark. I pull even with the driver. I look at him. I stop squinting. I open my eyes wide.

It's Elvis. The King.

He glances laconically at me, then stares, bored, ahead.

I know that what I am seeing is totally and utterly illogical and that it can't be real. I know he's been dead for years

and that even if he were alive, he'd be older than my dad
— but I swear to God, it's Elvis.

I decide to follow him. That if I don't follow him, I will
be missing a great and meaningful moment in my life —
even if it isn't real. That this is an opportunity not to be
refused. I coax my car along.

Elvis turns onto the bridge and heads across to another
side of town. Wherever he is going, he is in no particular
hurry. He is travelling exactly the speed limit. For some
reason, this bugs me. I think he should go faster. But why
should a dead man be in a hurry? What's the rush? Then
it occurs to me that a person in his condition doesn't need
to stop either — for anything, and what if he doesn't? What
if he goes all the way to Edmonton? Or Vancouver? Or
Nashville?

I begin to feel little nags of doubt, that maybe this isn't
such a good idea. That I should turn around and go home,
that this would be a far more reasonable thing to do and,
as a reasonable human being, this is what I should do. So
just as I take my foot off the gas, Elvis' signal light flashes.
He slows, and turns left onto a street I've never been on
before. We travel for a time through listless rows of houses.
It's so bright and clear that all the shabbiness is detailed
and accentuated. It would all look better if it was gray and
rainy.

But it is *windy*. Little dust devils twist about the boulevards
and a large cardboard box blows onto the street. Elvis takes
a wide berth around it. I follow.

We are in the middle of a nondescript grungy neighbourhood of clap-board and stucco houses built long before
I was born.

The Lincoln slows to a stop. I stop too. I suddenly get
very tense.

Elvis gets out of his car. He is dressed completely in black
— like he's supposed to be. He leans against the Lincoln

and takes out a package of cigarettes. He lights one up. He
glances over at me, then gazes at the stark prairie sky. I
didn't know Elvis smoked.

I've come this far. It would be stupid not to at least say
hi. I get out of the Toyota. I approach, my feet crunching
on the gritty asphalt. The wind is suddenly calm.

"Hi," I say, cheerily.

"How come y'all are following me?"

As soon as he speaks, I am immediately struck by two
things: the first is that this is definitely not Elvis, and the
second is that he sounds exactly like Elvis.

"I thought you were Elvis," I say.

His mouth flares into a kind of sneer. "A lot of people
think that," he drawls.

His mouth: his mouth definitely looks like Elvis'. I find
myself wishing for an instant that I was a girl. A girl would
know these things. I don't think I've ever looked at the
shape of somebody's mouth before.

"Well, are you?"

Elvis flicks his cigarette onto the road and grinds it into
the street with his pointy black boot. "Elvis's dead," says
Elvis.

"I know," I say. I'm not one of these people who believes
Elvis is alive.

"Well then, how can I be him?" The sneer reappears on
his mouth.

"You can't," I say, knowing that dead rock stars don't
drive through town in their Lincoln Continentals.

"That's right." He punctuates this with a kind of nod,
then looks off into the prairie sky again. "D'you know out
there was open prairie?" He indicates vaguely beyond the
tattered roofs. "Before that, it was a sea bed. And before
that, rock."

I have heard all this from my father. I am more interested
in what this Elvis is doing here.

I ask.

"I'm looking for someone," he says.

"Who?"

He does not answer me. I search his face for clues. Before I find any, he speaks again.

"Listen, young fellow, I got to go. I want to thank you for stopping to say hi." He says "thank" like it has a "g" on the end of it, instead of a "k". He climbs back into his car and slowly pulls away. His license plate says . . . Tennessee.

The Lincoln vanishes around a corner. I climb into my Toyota and begin my own journey. The large cardboard box we passed earlier is still in the middle of the street. I am thinking that if I accelerate the little Toyota through the box, I can send it flying out of the way — either that or it will lodge halfway beneath the car and I will have to remove it on my hands and knees. At the last moment, I swerve around the box, clipping it with the back of my bumper. I look through the rear-view mirror.

My heart stops as a small boy, maybe three years old, crawls out from the box. I jam on the brakes and jump out of the car. The boy is standing now. He gazes at me. His face is old. I know it is my dad.

By the time I arrive home, it is evening and Mom isn't there. The red light blinks on the answering machine. I press "playback".

"Kyle, please come to the hospital as soon as possible. Come straight up to the ICU." It's Mom. "ICU" is nursese for Intensive Care Unit.

When I get to the room, Mom is standing at the head of the bed. She is still wearing her nurse's uniform which means she hasn't been home for supper. She steps aside to reveal who is lying in the bed.

It's Dad.

I barely recognise him. He appears to be sleeping; his face is swollen, red. There is a tube going up his nose.

"He was hit by a car," says Mom.

"Where's Grandma?"

"She's coming."

We speak in those quiet conspiratorial tones that people use for these occasions, as though death does not like too much noise. I stare at the monitors and wonder how they work. I am wondering if they are giving life to Dad or if Dad is giving life to them.

I am not sure if time passes or if it is simply remaining still. But, by and by, Mom has gone for coffee and Grandma has arrived.

A man enters the room. He stops beside me at the head of the bed and looks at Dad. He looks at me.

It's Elvis.

"He is dying," Grandma says.

Elvis just stands there. Like he is trying to remember the words to a song.

Dad opens his eyes. He looks right at Elvis. "Hello," he says, "I haven't seen you in a long time."

"How do, Ray," says Elvis. He crosses to the side of the bed. He takes Dad's free hand. "How you feeling?"

"Not too good," says Dad.

"I'm glad I got here then. In time."

"In time for what?" I ask.

"To thank you, Ray. I want to thank you for jamming with me," he says.

Dad nods imperceptibly and smiles. He closes his eyes.

"You take care now," says Elvis. He softly releases Dad's hand. He nods at Grandma and I, then leaves the room.

◆◆◆

There are several strangers at the funeral who I assume are postal workers, as well as some man who sells geological supplies. Dad had been a good customer. There are no tears.

Mom stands beside me. I glance at her. She is staring down at the dirt and looks angry even though everything is willed to us. She would probably like to dump his rock collection on top of him.

Grandma, though, looks pleased. She is wearing a half-smile and is focusing on something deep inside her head. She is no doubt watching some secret vision.

Off in the distance, however, in the open field behind the cemetery, an old man is throwing a stick to a dog. The dog is a taffy-coloured mongrel. The old man is propped against an old bicycle. I stroll over there deciding just where I'm going to kick the old fart.

THE FRONT STEP

Vera had been raised on a small island in the Bay of Fundy where wild ponies once scuffled and yawned in the meadows. Vera often watched them feeding near the shore. Her favourite was a haughty roan filly that frisked and cantered and tossed her head like a duchess. She named her that — Duchess.

But the flies were relentlessly wicked the year the war ended. They tortured the small herd and chased them from the shore to the meadow and back. Vera watched the filly kick into the water, swim out into the channel, then disappear into the suck hole off the western point. Duchess was gone. The November before, Vera's father had sailed out past the same point to tend his traps. Neither did he return.

The first chance Vera got, she left the island. She was fifteen. Three years later, she found herself in Saskatoon — following a soldier she had met in St. John. But he went and married a farm girl from Delisle.

There never seems to be much choice about how you end up where you are. But when you find yourself there, you do one of two things: you stay, or you move on. If you stay, you have found something; if you move on, you are still looking.

So it was for Mr. Stanislav Warinek who found himself in Saskatoon just after the war as well. He was, in the lingo of the day, a DP, with nothing but a suitcase, his twenty-two years of past, and an address copied carefully onto the back of an envelope. DP meant *Displaced Person* and was a term used to describe any person who upset The Apparent Order of Things.

The address that Stanislav Warinek stared at, written on the envelope, belonged to a man who owned property in Saskatoon, a landlord whose heritage was the same as Stanislav's. He would give Mr. Stanislav Warinek a job and a place to stay.

It was not long before Stanislav was settled there. He began to work. And acquire things: a bicycle and a dog.

The Dog was a good dog. She was a taffy-brown mongrel who loved pulling rags in a tug of war with whomever would indulge her. When she wasn't doing that, she sat in a box on Stanislav's bike blankly smiling at passersby. Mr. Warinek fed The Dog canned Spam and would share a little picnic beside his bike where he ate bread and onions. The Dog would never go for the crumbs Stanislav dropped. She would kindly wait and let him do that.

It was only after he stood up, ready to return to work that The Dog would sniff out the picnic area for anything that remained. Then trot aside and piss, as dogs do.

Stanislav did odd jobs for the landlord. For that he received his room and fifteen dollars a week. He saved five of that fifteen to bring over his love from the old country. He had his dog and a bike. "Win, win; lose, lose: all the same thing," he would say, then fix an eave or patch a screen. Every month or so he received letters from his love's land, the old country, written in exotic script. They all began, "My Dearest Stanislav," and ended with, "I love you more than life." He would read them, hold them to his chest, and look down into the past. Then he would read them again, fold them, and carefully put them away with the others.

But the letters stopped coming. They simply stopped. Perhaps it was the politics, the Curtain of Iron. Perhaps it was something else. Stanislav didn't know. He waited, but nothing. The waiting and not knowing filled him with pain, the pain of dread.

One day he tore the mailbox off the wall as though the letters would somehow appear if the box was in his hand. Nothing. He wanted to kill the pain. He would drink it to death. He took ten dollars to the Albany Beverage Room and drank, the pain ebbing from him with each glassful of draught. He pissed on the sidewalk on the way home.

The next day he was still in pain, but this was easy pain, not the pain of waiting. He would wait no more. "Win, win; lose, lose: all the same thing."

The Dog was a good dog. He took her everywhere on the bike. He stopped one day for coffee at Lorne's Cafe on Twentieth Street. That was when Stanislav Warinek saw Vera for the first time. She was a waitress. She had eyes like a fawn. He was enchanted by them. He was soon in giddy love. He wrote to her, poems in the language of his birth. He wrote them, but never gave them to her. Vera couldn't have read them anyway. She couldn't read, in any language.

◆◆◆

It seemed to Vera there were many strange foreign men in Saskatoon. They dressed oddly and possessed indecipherable accents. They would come into Lorne's Cafe for coffee and toast and apple pie. They would speak to each other in tongues and laugh and roll cigarettes.

One of these strange men had a little taffy-coloured dog. It would sit in a box on his bicycle outside of Lorne's. The dog reminded her of home. She once had a dog named Queenie. The man would pat the dog, come inside and roll a cigarette. He would look at her and smile and nod and buy a cup of coffee. She could tell he wanted to talk to her, but was shy. Finally, she took pity on him.

"That your dog?"

"Yes. Yes." He nodded, smiling.

"I used to have one that looked just like her. What's her name?"

"No name. She just Dog."

"My dog's name was Queenie. You should call her Queenie."

"Qveenie. Qveenie. I like."

"She looks just like her."

"Qveenie. Very nice."

His smile filled her with something rich and strange. The Dog's name became Queenie. Stanislav became Stan.

They started going for walks, Vera, Stan and Queenie. Down by the river, back behind the Bessborough Hotel. They would stop from time to time and play with Queenie. They might have been brother and sister, but they were very soon lovers. They moved in together, into Stan's room.

That winter they took a night class at the Tech. They learned to read and write English. They pretended they didn't know each other in class and it was fun stealing glances across the room when the teacher asked a question.

That winter Stanislav Warinek took the letters he had put away and burned them all. He translated into English one of the poems he had written the previous fall.

> *I love you.*
> *I love you like a daughter and a mother and a queen.*
> *I love you like a country and I am a citizen.*
> *I love you like the sky and I am a star.*
> *I love you more than my life*
> *But that is not enough.*
> *I love you more than my death.*

♦♦♦

In the spring, Queenie had pups, six of them in her litter, all taffy-coloured, except one: it was white and black, a male and the largest in the litter. Queenie was a proud and good mother. She was no longer as interested in tugs of war. Vera fed her bread and milk. Stan got a job at the hospital, on the Maintenance Staff. Vera left Lorne's Cafe and began as a waitress at the Bessborough. She could now write on the order bill.

They all moved from the one room into a small house on Avenue T near the tracks. There was a ditch by the tracks filled with water where some neighbourhood children floated a raft. One of their neighbours kept chickens and sold their eggs. They were cheaper and fresher than at the store. There was a future. There was no past.

Perhaps it was time to think of children.

Queenie's litter grew. At four weeks, she moved them from the box behind the stove to a place under the front step. By six weeks most of the pups had been given away. Except the odd one, the big white and black male.

One day Queenie disappeared, taking with her the male pup. She returned a few hours later, alone. Stan was at work. Vera wondered where the pup had gone. She wandered near the tracks where some bigger boys were on the raft throwing rocks at something. They stopped when she got closer then jumped ashore and scattered like hens.

She saw what they were throwing rocks at: a small white and black rag that floated in the ditch. The puppy. Vera poked and pulled with a stick till she could reach it with her hand. She took it home and buried it in a corner in the back yard. When Stan returned from work, she told him that someone had come for the pup. That she'd given it away. Queenie hid in her place beneath the front step.

Vera worked on Saturdays while it was Stan's day off. He generally puttered around the yard and this day was trimming an overgrown lilac bush, very near the spot where Vera had buried the dog. Two things happened: first, Stan noticed the freshly turned earth. Then Queenie barked, at someone in the front yard.

The mailman came on Saturday's then, but he rarely stopped at Warinek's, seldom more than twice a month. So Stan was surprised when he saw the mailman leaving the front gate. He recognized immediately the handwriting on the envelope. His hands shook. The letter fluttered. He opened it and read. It began, "My Dearest Stanislav," and ended as the others had ended, "I love you more than life." He held it now, a still bird dead, unfolding. She would be coming. In two months, she would be here.

Stan was filled with pain and bewilderment. He went again to the Albany Hotel to empty the pain with glasses of draught. This time the pain survived, though there was no room for it. Vera came home to find Stan sleeping on the couch. He was snoring loudly, venting beer fumes. She woke him and he struggled to his feet. His mind was jumbled. He spoke in two languages. "All the same thing," was what she heard in English. He tried to hug her, but Vera stepped back and Stan fell onto the floor. He lay there and sobbed.

Vera went outside to get away from the crying man in the house. Queenie was nowhere in sight. She went around the back and saw where she had buried the pup. Instead of a patch of freshly turned earth, there was a hole. She went closer to examine it. The hole was not made with a shovel. It was a hole clearly dug by an animal. The dead pup was gone.

Stan lived in the drowned heavy silence of not knowing what to do. He would go to work, come home and sleep. The heaviness weighed on Vera. She wanted to help Stan, to cheer him up, but she didn't know how. She worried.

She might be with child. She grew frightened. How would she tell him? He would barely eat. He slept in fits and jumped every time Queenie barked.

Queenie had begun barking along the fence, as if irritated by passersby. She sat guarding the front step.

The water in the train ditch dried.

As the time for the arrival approached, there grew in the air a strange odour, the smell of rotting flesh. It grew stronger and stronger. The neighbour with chickens was blamed, but he pleaded innocence, indeed he counteraccused that someone was stealing his hens. Two of them, he said, had gone missing in the last two weeks alone. The stench got so bad that Stan emerged for a time to search its source. He was unable to find it.

A week before the arrival, a tempest flurried from the neighbour's henhouse. The neighbour came over saying he had seen their dog, Queenie, attacking his hens. One was dead and yet another was missing. The neighbour was dismissed. Queenie was a good dog. She seldom strayed from the yard. She would not behave like that.

But the next morning some feathers and a trail of blood soaked into the board sidewalk told the truth. The trail led to a small hole underneath the front step. Crouched on his knees, Stan knew now the stench's source. He tore the step apart, heaving and ripping boards with a crowbar. There, lying in a corner, were two rotting hens — a third was freshly killed — plus the putrid remains of a white and black pup.

Stan's thinking suddenly became very clear. He shoveled the corpses into a box and cremated them in the back yard with the lumber torn from the step. He paid the neighbour for the lost hens. He bought new lumber from Ball's and fixed the step. He did all this without uttering a word.

Then he bought a gun, a twelve-gauge shotgun and a box of shells, from Eatons.

With the gun and shells still wrapped in the paper from the store, he took Queenie for a walk out onto the prairie and shot her.

One of the big boys found the near-full box of shells together with the dog and gun. The police were called. There was no sign of Stan. He'd simply vanished. Perhaps he would turn up. Perhaps he'd gone to the river. He might have caught a freight train west. Or east. Vera didn't know. Only that he loved her more than death. Six days after she had reported him missing, Vera packed all Stan's things into boxes and gave them to the Salvation Army. She wore mourning black.

On the seventh day a cab pulled up in front of the house. A woman got out. She went to the door but no one was home. She got her bags, both of them, and set them on the new front step. She waited.

When Vera returned from work she found a strange woman dresed in strange clothes curled up asleep in front of the door. Vera woke her. They looked into each other's eyes and for a moment there was fear.

"I am looking for Stanislav Warinek," the woman said.

Vera invited her in.

PRINTED AND BOUND
IN BOUCHERVILLE, QUÉBEC, CANADA
BY MARC VEILLEUX IMPRIMEUR INC.
IN OCTOBER, 1997